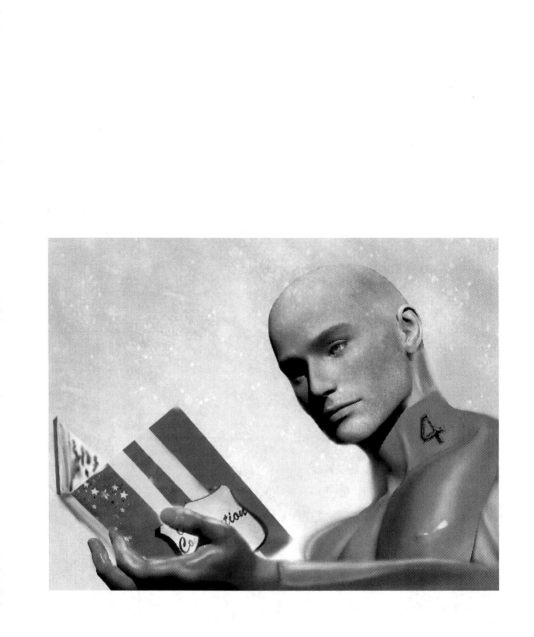

SILVERSUIT III

~ Heritage ~

BY

B. PALMA

Artwork, photography
and art modifications by
Imad Obegi – Illustrator

authorHOUSE®

AuthorHouse™ LLC
1663 Liberty Drive
Bloomington, IN 47403
www.authorhouse.com
Phone: 1-800-839-8640

Published by AuthorHouse 07/18/2014

ISBN: 978-1-4969-1864-2 (sc)
ISBN: 978-1-4969-1863-5 (e)

Library of Congress Control Number: 2014910876

Certain stock imageries are courtesy of Dreamstime©. Any people depicted in stock imagery provided by Dreamstime© are models, and such images are being used for illustrative purposes only.

The photographs of "Cato" and the author, and modification designs on covers and other interior illustrations are by Imad Obegi, illustrator. Imad@obgillustrator.com

This book is printed on acid-free paper.

Also by the author:

The Secret of the Haunted Hacienda

Lucifer

The Mystery of the Tarascan Ruins

The Monarch Mystery

10 Horses and a Pony

El Dorado

Love's End

And Then

Silversuit (Series I, II and III)

Written under her professional name,
Beverley Blount M.Ed:

The Blount Guide to Reading, Spelling and
Pronouncing English

Contact author at her web page and blog:

www.paloalto-bilingual-adventures.com

To Imad Obegi with many thanks
for his amazing art work.

ACKNOWLEDGEMENTS

To Mariana Calvo for her intuitive ideas for the text and to Beth Argus for hers on the illustrations.

Table of Contents

Chapter 1

The Coloring Book

Wrapping her old blanket over her head to cover the lumps in her wool ski cap, L'ora slipped out of the transit pod and, bent over, shuffled toward the down ramp. Moving close to the protecting wall she reached the bottom of the ramp and faced the swirling winds. A quick look around confirmed no one else had dared this unseasonal blizzard and she braved the driving sleet to dash across the promenade. Tattered and damp banners streamed in the blizzard's tormenting scream and the broken and ruined decorations decried the cancellation of the day's festivities, the beginning of the weeklong worldwide holiday.

Holding tightly onto the banister, L'ora climbed the few icy steps of her building and slipped and slid to the nearest access portal. Pulling her standard issue ring through the slit in her threadbare gloves, she pressed its crest into the round slot and quickly eased through the misty opening in the frame. *It's just as cold in here but at least I'm out of the freezing wind*, she thought and raced toward the nearest lift portals. Keying her ring, she stepped into the waiting pod and clung to the handles as its clear panel wrapped around her. Barely giving her time to catch her breath, the pod lifted and swiftly raced into the myriad of tubes whose octopus tunnels wove all over the huge residential complex.

As the pod whistled through the tubes L'ora closed her eyes and again kept the panic at bay by thinking of her famous Great-Great Gran's stories of her youth when sellers used similar pods to send their money markers from the credit cashers to the central offices.

The pod finally shrieked to a stop and the clear panel slid around her and opened onto an empty hall. L'ora rushed out and turned to her right to begin jogging down the chilly corridor. She stopped for a second to check the large crack in the frame for she no longer tried to keep track of the latest code number of her floor. Pulling her blanket around her, she faced the whistling drafts and dashed down the hall. Running past the long "N" corridor to her left and the next eleven corridors, she reached the end of the hall. There she turned into the smallest corridor and headed toward the threshold of the only frame on the right hand side. Her "Z" corridor, wedged into the south side of the building, barely fitted her cubicle and the two frames in front marked "Storage" and "Maintenance." At the threshold of her portal, she ringed her access circle and stepped into her room, the space in her frame misting behind her. One step brought her to the C.H.A.R. parallel to the frame wall.

"Cato, your mistress is home," L'ora said, lifting her lightweight inside jumpsuit off the furry body curled tightly against the cold. Picking up the fawn-colored cat, she gave it a soft rub and laid it back down, covering it with the general issue blanket. "I'm so sorry I had to take the blanket Cato, but it's just too cold outside. I don't think anyone else went to work today, not at the beginning of Constitution Week."

L'ora hung her waterproof carrysak on the side of her C.H.A.R and opened it to peek inside, assuring her treasures were safely there. Stepping over to her cabinet, she pulled out a soup container and measured a full ration of cat food into Cato's bowl. "Here Kitty, Kitty," she said, putting the bowl down under the blanket and setting her soup to heat.

Stripping off her outside coverall, she pulled on her jumpsuit, shivering as the inadequate material gave her little protection. She left the soft wool ski cap pulled over her head, mentally thanking Great-Great Gran for her long ago gift.

Hanging up the heavier outside coverall on a wall peg, she grasped her soup and stretched out beside the cat. Nudging the controls at her shoulder she watched the transparent pod closing over her. Her shivering skin bathed in the warm air eddying from the Controlled Heating And Recliner.

L'ora relaxed and sipped the hot soup, luxuriating in the first minutes of a week's holiday. Cato finished his bowl and curled onto her lap while she finished hers. "We're getting an added bonus credit for the holidays," she said, "so we can stock up on a few extra rations."

Triggering the 3D wall newscast, she watched the Supreme Master Professor speaking to the world. Extolling the brilliance of the Founders who wrote the famous Constitution, he expounded at length, portraying their importance as the center of the weeklong yearly celebration. Several Master Teachers stood behind him, nodding their heads at certain pertinent comments.

His mysterious silver-suited protectors flanked his sides; their skin shimmering with the silver covering enclosing their bodies. The shining muscles of their strong arms and legs were easily visible through the glimmering paper-thin covering. Their faces were expressionless, stern and handsome.

I wonder if their Silverskin makes them as powerful as rumors tell, she thought.

L'ora slipped her hand into her carrysak to find her treasure, a page-sized pamphlet. "Look Cato, as archivist, I was able to find the actual written words of the Constitution. I wonder why I could find nothing else except this, hidden in a children's coloring book called *Laws.*"

Bending her knees, she propped the thin book against her legs and on the uncomplaining cat. Turning the first page, L'ora began to read. *It's strange to actually read something written on paper.*

Chapter 2

Silversuiters

Three times L'ora read the small book. Perplexed, she looked at Cato, "This is something so different from what we were taught. These rules give power to everyone, not just the Teachers. During the celebrations, why doesn't anyone read them instead of learning the lives of those who wrote them? Why do we celebrate something not being used?"

Cato looked past her with wide turquoise eyes. With a long "M-e-o-w", he jumped off her lap, under the pod cover, and dashed through the back portal onto the emergency walkway surrounding every floor of each compound.

"Cato, come back!" . . . Trying to catch him, she leaned under the pod cover, almost slipping onto the floor.

A strong blast of wintery air blew across her back and, with a feeling of disaster, she turned to the now opened portal of her frameway and gasped at the sight of the two muscular Silversuiters standing there.

"How did you open my frame and what do you want?" she said, her heart pounding with fright.

"Herdez, get the cat before it warns a neighbor," commanded the taller Silversuiter. His sturdy companion saluted, crossing the stiff fingers of each hand to lie on the biceps of the other arm. Turning, he raced around the C.H.A.R toward the outside portal, his plated arm held out before him.

"Yes Sir, Commander Fourth, I'll be right back."

Fourth watched Herdez's disappearing figure, *He wouldn't dare mock my new command*, he thought.

Looking fiercely at the C.H.A.R. and the figure covered by the blanket, he said, "L'eo R'oaks, you are under arrest for taking unauthorized material from the archives."

"N-no," she managed to say with just her eyes showing over the old blanket. "I'm Head Archivist for the Sixth Zone as my father and grandfather were. I'm allowed to revise unclassified material. See, this is a child's coloring book but it has the original words of the Constitution."

Fourth snatched the booklet from where it had slipped off her lap and began leafing through it.

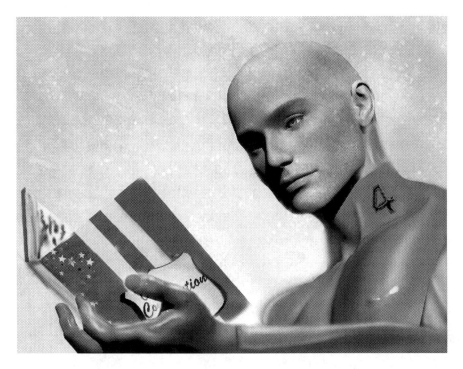

". . . This is heresy, it can't be the original."

He started reading it in earnest, only noticing in time L'ora's attempt to slip around him and dart through the frame to the corridor. Reaching out a long silver arm, he grabbed her wrist, pulling her around before him.

The opened frame misted shut behind her.

When his hand touched her, suddenly her body no longer obeyed her. Each muscle followed *his* body's commands as thousands of painful pinpricks ran up and down her skin. As if a robot, she marched up to him, her mind begging her to flee but her muscles only responded to the orders of *his* nervous system.

Make your captives totally subservient; the words from the training manual said. His fingers ordered her right hand to creep up her shoulders and unlatch the catches of her jumpsuit, causing it to slip down to her feet as he ripped away the sleeve of the arm he held. Reaching out, the Silversuiter snatched the non-issue wool covering from her head.

Gasping in astonishment, he watched as long waves of red hair pulled out of the wool and flowed down her shoulders and back. He pushed her back against the C.H.A.R. and stared in amazement. "Great Gaia! You're a girl!" he said, "What deceit is this? How have you managed to avoid the laws to keep your head shaven? When I turn you in, you will be tried and sentenced to painful tortures by the Tenured Professors."

Chapter 3

Interrogation

For a long moment Fourth stared at her. He looked up and down at her body plastered against the C.H.A.R. "How old are you?" He asked.

"T-today's my twentieth birthday," she answered, her teeth chattering in fear and cold.

"Good. Then you became of age and I can interrogate you."

"Why haven't you shaved your head?" . . . "Why are your clothes so ragged?"

Staring in terror at him, she couldn't answer, the violent actions of the Silversuiters portrayed on the glass wallcast raced through her mind.

Her arms wrapped around herself, inadequately trying to protect her body against the cold.

Fourth stepped closer. "Why do you keep your room so cold?" He looked around and touched his hands to her waist. Pulling her close, he held her legs against his, bonding them together. His silver hands on her waist and the pressure of his thumbs forced her to bend back, her waves of hair hanging down where they would not touch his body. His legs controlled hers and she found herself making awkward backward steps toward the frame beside them. He extended his wrist plate and the opaque shadow within the closed frame disappeared, revealing her bed cubicle. Her body moved toward the thin mattress, her legs and arms following commands of nerves not her own. The back of her legs touched the frame and he picked her up by her waist and lobbed her against the unfinished rough plasticrete that walled the cubicle. She cried out, her freed nerves feeling the painful scratches raking across her bare skin.

Fourth slid in beside her, the frame misting behind him. For a long moment he stared at her.

"You don't weigh anything, you shouldn't have hit so hard," he said as if despite his rank, he was repenting having thrown her so hard.

Ripping off a piece of the bed sheet, Fourth indicated L'ora should wrap it around her hair. He hesitated, then leaned forward and put his hands on her shoulders, pulling her to a kneeling position in front of him.

"Come to me L'eo," he said, kneeling in front of her, his shaved head almost touching the top of the cubicle. Pressing her chest against his, he tried to kiss her but her face and lips did not meld into his raw face skin as the rest of her body was doing under the control of her nerves through his Silverskin. His hands slipped down her arms and commanded them to hug him closer. Her mind resisted but her body obeyed his and her arms opened out and hugged his wide shoulders against her.

L'ora struggled, her head being the only part of her not controlled by his silver-tinted skin. Pulling her lips away from his, she jerked her head aside. A long red strand of hair escaped the sheet, whipping around his neck and, surprised, she saw the silver disappear from around his neck.

Pulling back and sitting on his heels Fourth looked at her in amazement as his fingers touched the bare skin of his neck and the shaved skin behind it. "You witch, what have you done to my Silversuit?" he said, his face flushed in anger.

Frightened, and feeling the mysterious bonds between them disappear, L'ora slipped back against the rough wall beside her pillow. The puffs of warm air heating her bed cubicle lifted tendrils of her freed hair and the red strands floated around her face.

Fourth started to speak but stopped as he gazed at the frightened girl stretched against the wall. "You're the most beautiful woman I've ever seen, why were you not searched for the Teacher's Lounge? Is this more of your magic?" He reached out and touched her leg, transmitting again his power over her.

L'ora drew in her breath before answering, "N-no one ever goes into the archives. My dad registered me as his apprentice when I was eleven, just as his father did with him. When my registration came it said L'eo, my father's name, and he said not to change it. When the Center Archive sent me word the bacteria had invaded his lungs and killed him, I was appointed in his place. No one came to check when I registered and was sent my new card and ring."

Fourth looked at her and reached for her waist. "If I turn you in, you will be severely punished by the Tenured Teacher's Council for breaking the laws in so many ways."

"I haven't, I just read the real Constitution and I have done nothing wrong." she said in protest.

He looked at her in amazement. "Where did you get a true copy, no one has ever seen one."

"This one is a child's coloring book and shows in pictures with titles of the entire Constitution and some amendments. It's very old, the date says 1955, and the access code is my grandfather's."

Fourth loosened his belt and pulled his long tunic over his head. His strong chest and powerful muscles glowed silver grey in the pale light of the cubicle. Then he leaned forward and his hands grasped her waist. "By the oldest Silversuit laws, you are mine to protect."

She thought of grabbing the mattress but her body followed his commands, pulling her toward him. "If you toss your head, I will turn you in, and you will be sent to the Consequentors when the Tenures finish with you."

L'ora cringed when she heard the dreaded title said aloud. She had never heard it uttered except in terrified whispers. It was said no one in their grasp had ever returned to tell their tale.

He ripped another piece of the sheet and threw it over her hair, using it to pull her until she was again kneeling in front of him. He breathed into her mouth. "Kiss me back."

She felt her entire body reaching for him but his kisses brought no reply from her unresponsive mouth against his tanned face and she twisted her head away.

"Kiss me," he repeated, his voice frightening her as her body became totally controlled by his, causing his waves of desire to course into her deepest being. A silver finger brushed her lips and around her mouth, touching their lips together. His kisses now became fire racing through her shaking body and her mind was the only part of her not aching to match his desire. She knew nothing about what her body was doing and the wild desire she felt was something unknown to her; her years of hiding from any observer had not prepared her for the intense contact of a male body's desires.

L'ora looked at his face as she felt his desire flowing over her entire body. *He's a Silversuit Commander, how is it that he wants me so? I'm just an archivist.* His desire spread across her and his need of her included her responding to his feelings. She found her arms wrapping around him and pulling her against his body.

She looked down at him where he was kneeling in front of her and gasped, "You're deformed, a monster!"

For a moment Fourth didn't realize why she had called him a monster until he looked down at himself. "Are you crazy? I'm a man who wants you. Don't you know anything about men and women? The Manual says all women will beg to come to a Silversuiter hoping to prove they are not barren. You must know something, answer me!" His commands ran through her synapses into forgotten memories in her brain.

"M-my dad never told me anything except to never let a man get close enough to discover I was a woman and to hide until my twentieth coming of age."

L'ora paused for a minute, quivering; long embedded sights and scenes projected into her consciousness and thrust unwillingly into speech.

"Once, when I was just in my teens, my father got permission to take me to my Great-Great Gran's when she was dying. He covered my head and dressed me like a boy." She faltered, but continued under the commands sweeping through her nervous synapses. "I was sent to walk while they talked and saw a horse with part of him stretched out looking the way you are. He was neighing and snorting with his head in the air and his nose pulled back. He started galloping and leaped over a high fence and ran toward another horse. I thought they were going to fight and he reared up as if he was attacking the other but it didn't move as he reared onto it. I didn't understand what they were doing but I realized it was a female and what it did to her didn't seem to hurt her. It made me feel funny to watch them . . . as I do now." She shuddered, "A-are you going to do that to me?" Her memory bewildered her even more and she couldn't help looking down at him.

With a fervent gaze, the Silversuiter pulled L'ora against him and tipped her back, his body pressing against her. "Yes, and you will like it."

Fourth's demanding words and desire sent tremors though her as her body melded against him. Desire flowed from his nerves through her nervous system, unleashing uncontrolled responses and causing his waves of desire to run through her deepest being. His lips touched hers again, awaking flaming feelings that raced through her searching body. An uncertain fear in her mind was the only part of her not craving him as her body wildly mirrored everything he desired. Then her mind lost all control and every nerve in her body connected to his demanding force.

Chapter 4

Trapped

Their movements joined and she felt tingles over her entire body as she echoed him, pulling him closer to her. He sighed in her ear and she mirrored his ecstasy as her body wildly responded and matched his movements.

L'ora knew she was moaning *his* pleasure, but her mind projected confusion and fear although the ecstatic feeling of his wild release never stopped.

They lay together after and Fourth gazed into her face and covered her lips with kisses. "Don't you know anything about love?" he said.

Her body still trapped within his control, she felt tears streaming down her cheeks and pain in the inner reaches of her body. "Only what I've been allowed to read by the censorship," she whispered, feeling desire again running from his nerves into hers. "Please . . . you're hurting me," she started to say but his control of her body did not allow her to say anything else and his wild desire again caused her to moan and respond as her arms grasped him close. His silver finger began to play with her body, laughing as she trembled in response to his electric caresses. He again joined their bodies together for what seemed an impossible time until she collapsed, exhausted and gasping for breath.

He drew away from her and left her spent body limp on the sheets. "Do not move, you know the consequences; Herdez is back and you must not make a sound." Throwing on his long tunic and fastening its belt, he opened the frame and slipped through as it closed behind him.

She breathed small sighs into the pillow and did not try to leave the cubicle.

"Where's the cat?" Fourth said, looking at Herdez.

"It's coming, I chased it all the way around to the north side. It jumped up on the railing and then to a cornice where I couldn't reach it. I finally gave up and started back and the blasted animal just jumped down and passed me, stopping to look back as if telling me to follow it. It stopped for a minute outside to sniff a crack and there it is now."

Cato stalked in, the black tip of his faun tail flicking back and forth in distain. He royally ignored the two men and, obligingly opened by his collar, he jumped through the open bed frame.

Herdez gasped at the quick sight of the uncovered legs lying limply on the rumpled sheets. "Commander, I didn't know, you didn't tell me."

For an instant Fourth didn't understand his implications but quickly grasped his chance. Putting his arm around Herdez's shoulder he replied, "Well, I wasn't sure about you, either."

Herdez slipped out from his grasp, saying, "You should meet Robert and Roland, the heads of security for the Master Teachers' Lounge. All security guards there must have a partner before being assigned to the compound. They get more perks than anyone else. Would you like for me to introduce you?"

Fourth smiled and winked toward the bed frame, "Not right now, I think I've found someone who will keep me occupied during this entire vacation . . . Look, I had my pass with transportation and lodging to visit the Barren's village over the tree line in zone 50, but I find it more interesting to stay right here. Would you like to take it? You might find someone to amuse you there or even a permanent partner if you can get her pregnant."

"Aren't you going to arrest him?"

"No, why? Her...his papers are in order as Division Sixth Head Archivist and what he took was just an unclassified child's coloring book teaching the laws." He winked again, "Of course, I'm not going to tell him, he'll be afraid enough to follow my slightest command."

Herdez grinned and looked at the pass, "Thanks, I'll certainly enjoy this, you must have greatly pleased someone with your work to get a turn so soon. I won't get mine for a long time."

Fourth smiled back, "Good, but let's keep this a secret. I don't want anyone spoiling my vacation or afterwards reassigning me. And you don't want anyone to know you took my place. Here's the Manual for first timers. Now hurry or you'll miss the next pod shuttle."

Herdez started to clap his superior on his shoulder but stopped, grinned, and activated the frame leading out into the frigid drafts.

Fourth heard him running down the hall and waited until his footsteps faded away. Then he picked up her ski cap and the thin booklet from the floor and headed toward the bed frame.

Chapter 5

Reading

L'ora lay where he had left her and Fourth's eyes devoured her as he climbed through the frame. *She's so beautiful, she's bewitched me. I can't think of anything but my desire to hold her again. That dangerous hair, why does it attract me so?* He put her head covering into her hand and said, "Put it on and tuck your hair under it."

She sat up against the wall and managed to cover her hair with the soft wool. As soon as she tucked the last strand in, he touched her hand, "Come here," he said. Propping her pillow on the rough plasticrete and sitting against it, he stretched his long legs across the torn sheets.

Fourth wrapped one arm around her and pulled her beside him, holding her close. "Now, let's read this so-called Constitution."

Her brain told her to struggle to try to run away but her body remained under the control of his nerve endings and, trembling, she was pressed against his silver skin as he began to read.

After the third time he read it, his face changed. "How could we celebrate this document without following it?" For a moment his control abated and she pulled out of his grasp and rolled out of the bed frame, crashing on the floor and sprinting out of her kneeling position.

He jumped out and dashed after her, grabbing her before she reached the hall frame. He pulled her to him, holding her arms and marching her back to the bed cubicle. Picking her up, he tossed her onto the thin mattress. Ducking under the top of the frame, he threw himself on her.

"You dare to defy a Silversuiter! That's forbidden! You'll burn with the consequences right now! I'll make you feel what else my nerves can do to you!" He rubbed his hand against her, every touch a burning ember.

L'ora cried out and looked at him, "Stop," she pleaded. Surprised, she saw him spring back, still holding her wrist.

"Witch, you hurt me! My skin is burning!" He looked at her in amazement, "I felt what I was doing to you and am feeling your pain and fear and the feeling that I will keep on burning you. You're afraid I will repeat what we just did. This can't be happening, Silverskin *never* reflects a captive's feelings back to a Silversuiter. What I did to you is now hurting me. Didn't you enjoy me as I did you? You should have felt what I felt. You responded as if with great pleasure . . . The manual says all women do and ask for more. I can't believe what I did with you was so painful. Is it the reason some people run away from Silversuiters? They should know a Silversuiter would not hurt a possibly fertile woman." He paused, "But I just did, . . . you disobeyed me and I hurt you in anger." He looked into her eyes. "You fear me and with great reason. I have done something I swore never to do."

Fourth reached inside a pouch that rested on the side of his tunic. "Here," he said, reaching toward her. "This will help the pain."

L'ora shied away from his hand but he held her arm and began to rub a silvery cream into her scratches. Frightened, she felt his desire awaken as he touched her.

"Please, no," she said, trembling.

"Don't be afraid, this won't hurt." Fourth began to rub the shining cream over her body and she felt the pain disappearing wherever he touched. She could no longer feel the deep scratches on her back and when he rubbed it on each side of her forehead, she felt her fears slip away and the mistrust being eased from her mind. As he massaged her body, his fingers became caresses, smoothing away her pain and touching softly her most sensitive parts as he felt her responses begin to reflect into him. He turned her over and his fingers slowly covered her skin with the silver cream while his nerves broadcast a questioning desire, as if begging her to forgive him and to respond with feelings from her heart. He cradled her in his arms, sending deep thoughts of tenderness and caring into her nervous system that ultimately caused her to lean against his chest as if accepting his protection and friendship after so many years of loneliness. The pain and fear she had just experienced seemed to disappear as his feelings of caring spread through her body.

Her eyes searched his, "You won't hurt me again? You will hold me and never leave me alone?" She rubbed her hand over the strong muscles of his arm and chest. "Can I depend on you?"

He kissed her softly again and again until her lips began to respond with a desire all of her own and her body reached toward him to join their nerve centers with equal yearnings.

Again he covered her, this time projecting caring feelings instead of pain and dominant commands. At first fearfully, her body began to respond, her arms and legs timidly pulling him toward her. Each felt the other's most pleasurable spots and their bodies responded with a mutual desire to please the other. She felt no pain as he entered her, only the knowledge of their combined needs and they moved united, each feeling and responding to the other's most sensitive and responsive areas until together they cried as one and fell back on the pillow in exhausted pleasure.

They rested and he spoke first, "No couple could ever have felt a double pleasure like this before. I felt yours and mine at the same time. You truly are magic."

He lifted up on one elbow and leaned over to kiss her but pulled back in shock. "No, it can't be, there has never been a female Silversuiter!"

L'ora looked in amazement at the soft tendrils of silver that were creeping toward her stomach and she felt a warm tingling over and inside her entire body. Regardless of all he had done to her, her fear of him disappeared and she looked into his eyes with a courage and confidence she had never known. "You will protect me."

He gathered her against him and whispered in her ear. "I don't know if this is what the old books meant but I think I'm in love with you. I want you to be with me for always. After what I did, how can you want me to be yours? I promise to protect you and never hurt you again."

She smiled, still wondering about her courage. "I think perhaps you'd better tell me your name first."

He paused, then said, "It's been so very long since anyone has mentioned my name, I'd almost forgotten it. I remember I was named Scott but my Mom called me Scotty before she was taken."

Chapter 6

Changes

Scott tried to cover them with the shredded sheets and complained, "Why do you have your bed cubicle at such a low temperature?" He reached into his pouch again and brought out some tokens and started to feed them into the slots above the thermometer.

L'ora grabbed his hands, "No, they know how many credits I have, I can't suddenly have more marks than before. I wouldn't have spent my entire Constitution bonus on heating. I can't afford to be investigated and now you can't either. They'll come and take you away and send me to the Council to do their wishes and I'll be unprotected again."

"Don't worry, L'eo, I won't leave you or let anyone take you." He held her in his arms and rocked her against him. When she relaxed, he looked at her. "What about your shower? Is it also icy cold?"

She nodded, "But I might have spent one of my bonuses for a special hot bath."

"Come, let's do exactly that."

They ran through the icy room into the tiny necessities cubical where she folded all the appliances into the wall and pulled out the long tube with the 'fone' head. "I always wondered why it was called a 'fone,' what's a fone?"

"Never thought about it. I have no idea."

She looked at him and caught her breath while tears ran down her cheeks. She sobbed great gulping sobs as she clung against him.

Her uncontrollable spasms of crying went on and on. He tried to comfort her with words and hugs. "What's the matter? . . . Don't cry . . . Is it what I did?"

She gulped and finally was able to speak, "You're the first person I've talked to openly face to face in almost five years. I always sit in the single back seat on the public pods and avoid everyone else. Although this complex used to have people, I haven't seen anyone on this floor for a long time and the pods don't carry many people over this way any more. I try to talk to people on the wallcast of the archives room but have to tell them that the vision is faulty. Since there aren't many repair people, no one comes to fix it and people always believe me. They don't know I never put in a request. Once I thought I had a friend but it kept questioning me and I used the questions that Dad told me to use and realized it was an inspecting machine."

He folded her into his arms, "Well, talk to me as much as you please . . . But where will you put me and how will we broadcast the real Constitution all over the world?"

"Put you . . . to live here? Broadcast? What are you talking about? How can I come out of hiding? They'll separate us."

He fed tokens into the red dotted slot and turned on the water, spraying them both with the hot stream. She hung her wool head covering on a small hook and enjoyed more hot water than she could ever remember using. Her long hair streamed flat in the spray he projected on her and another token ejected a perfumed shampoo that covered her head in luxurious suds.

"Be careful," Scott said, "don't brush up against me."

L'ora shook her head, rinsing away the suds and knotting the long waves in a frayed towel.

He gathered her into his arm and rinsed the suds off of their bodies, the water flowing off into the recycle drain.

"I don't have another towel, what shall you do?"

"Don't worry, water flows quickly off Silverskin. I'll just dry my face on the top of your towel." He nuzzled his face down on her towel, then looked at her, "L'eo, your Silverskin hasn't covered very much of you, but just touching my fingers over those tendrils of silver threads on your stomach drives me mad with desire."

"L'ora," she corrected, "I'm named after my great-great grandmother. Gran and her husband were the first to realize what was happening with the women going barren and what the bacteria was doing to the men and they started the hero teachers protecting the children. They saved thousands of children from being kidnapped by barren families and thieves that realized that children were the most expensive commodities in the world. Great-great-gran outlived the next two world generations, even those living in the ice cities."

Fourth looked puzzled, "That's strange, I remember when I was very small my mom told me some of that story and said that someone in our family had been in that group of protectors. I don't know much more because she was taken and the bacteria got my father soon after so I was taken to see if the Silverskin would accept me and then start my warrior training."

"Why did you ask me how we were going to broadcast and where you were going to stay? My place is tiny and of course I have no electronics."

"We'll worry about that later, right now I'm starved. What do you have to eat?"

Again she looked upset. "Food? I hardly have anything for you. Cato and I live on the minimum basic rations." Seeing him reach into his pouch again she grabbed his hand. "No, you can't get food here, even with my bonus, I would not have enough for you to eat." She touched his arm and, her curiosity aroused, she looked at the soft suede covering bonded to his forearm. "Can this open all frames?"

His face reflected his pride, "This one can open all the frames in the world. History says that there are only five wrist controls known that can do that and I am the youngest Silversuiter to have one. Our world Brain Center has two more and no one knows where the others are." His face changed as he remembered,

"My Master Silversuit Trainer First was one and when I managed to find him after the avalanche, he passed his to me before he died. Once the control accepts you, it's yours for life and you become a sworn Protector of the Supreme Master Professor. All Silversuiters live long lives and Silversuit Master First was in his late 90's. I felt as though he was my real father, and I was his special protégé. That terrible afternoon I *felt* him call me and dug him out from the snow where boulders had trapped and broken his body. He died in my arms." He held her tightly; "I don't know why I'm saying this, I've never talked about Master Silversuiter First to anyone."

She looked at him and hugged him back. *Such a strong man and he's got tears in his eyes.* "Now I know what to do. Come, Dad and Granddad lived across the hall, maybe you can get in, and there I think you can still order something beside basic." She looked down at herself, "And maybe something for me to wear."

"Why didn't you go in and get what you needed?"

"The rings only open to the places assigned for them and they never sent me Dad's back. I've never been in there before; he wouldn't let me in, saying it wasn't safe. I'm sure he thought that if something happened to him I would have his ring to live better." She frowned, "His ring could open my door and the archive rooms." Her face reflected her pain as she remembered reading the short notice posted to her on the wallcast.

Archivist L'eo R'oaks, we hereby inform you of the death of your father, Leonardo R'oaks. His body has been cared for properly.

You will take his place as Division Six Head Archivist and your ring and certificate will reach you shortly.

He held her close, both remembering the deaths of their fathers and the disappearances of their mothers.

Chapter 7

The Storage Room

L'ora peeked through the frame and down the 'Z' corridor then turned back into Scott's arms. "What's the matter"" he asked, then realized that she was turning blue with cold. "Here", he said, reaching into his pouch and bringing out a gossamer silver cape. Putting it over her shoulders, he said, "How something so thin can keep you warm I don't know but it will surely help."

She wrapped it around her and then slipped out, followed by Scott. She pointed to the frame marked 'Storage'.

"Here's Dad's frame and the one down the corridor toward the window was Granddad's." Looking at him hopefully, she whispered, "Can you open it?"

He smiled at her and confidently walked through the frame that misted silently before him. She quickly followed and he turned to her, "See, no problem."

A screeching alarm ripped away his words as they both spun around to see red lights flashing through the room. "Quick," he said, "look for a hand plate on the walls."

She had already spotted the one beside the frame and ran to it, placing her palm on it and looking into the tiny red beams that shot into her eyes.

The alarm stopped before he reached her. "I thought you said you had never been here before?"

"Dad had a plate like this on one of the archive rooms, the one I had never been able to access until today. He must have keyed this one for me, thinking that I would have his ring if anything happened to him."

They turned to look into the room, the red light slowly changing into a warm glow that outlined the affluent furnishings around them. The wide C.H.A.R. in the middle would easily fit two and the ornate bed and necessities frames were large and made of carved wood; a luxury she had never seen. The food counter was wide with high stools facing a u-shaped part extending out into the large room. For a minute they just looked around and then L'ora pulled at his arm, "Scotty, it's warm in here! How can that be if no one has put any credit marks in?"

He didn't answer; his attention focused on the wide desk under the silvery wall covering that was the wallcast. He walked over and started touching the desk, its top a glowing mirror that offered a multitude of choices for inquisitive fingers. He turned and grabbed her, "You lied to me, your father didn't die five years ago, this desk has advanced circuitry beyond any used by the highest level of the Tenured Council." He shook her, "Why did I believe you? No one ever dares to lie to a Silversuit, we always feel their lies."

She stuttered, "I, I did tell you the truth, I've never been in here before. Dad always told me that I could come in on my 20th birthday but not before. He said his knowledge was dangerous for me and being poor would protect me. I guess he never thought that I would not have his ring."

He looked into her eyes. "I think you told me the truth but where did all this equipment come from?"

"I don't know, Granddad hardly ever went to work with us, I was doing his filing work from the time I was ten. Even Dad sometimes left me and I ran the whole office, especially after Granddad died. There wasn't much work, we filed any papers that came through; since paper was so dear, mostly we used the archive terminals and just checked that the central controls placed the electronic files in the right archives according to their titles. I had lots of time to read but could not open many of the articles I filed. It was one of those days that Dad never came back."

He let go of her and eagerly turned to the CG-glass top of the desk. Touching certain spots, the clear top programed a 3D hologram of him holding and shaking her that filled the entire surface of the wallcast. He reached out one long leg and pulled the desk chair up. Sitting on a corner of its cushion, his fingers raced over the surface and many text boxes filled with words and holograms covered where their figures had been. Then everything disappeared and the angled face of a man with close-cropped silver hair appeared on the wallcast.

"Fourth, what feast will you have for today?" said the young/old man with a knowing grin. "Your most highly-educated 'intellectual' bosses planning another meditative retreat with some of the select members of the Master Teacher's Lounge?"

Scott smiled but shook his head. "This time it's for me, Jôn, and I want a complete number four with your best bubbly for two people. My Silversuit Master First said I could always trust you and I want you to see the reason why." He pulled L'ora against him, focusing the transmission on their heads and necks to avoid showing the torn remnants of her clothing through the almost transparent cloak.

"Great Gardens of Gaia! Man, you've got a Palmer with you! I thought they had all been hunted down, questioned, and turned over to the Consequentors! I'm going on closed beam right now and you do the same." His face disappeared from the screen and reappeared in a small box in one corner of the huge silver wall.

Chapter 8

The Bonding

A picture of a young woman in boots and ancient riding clothes came up in another small box and L'ora exclaimed in surprise, "That's Great-Great-Grandmother, she actually rode horses for pleasure before the Maelstrom."

Scott looked at the face on the wall, "She was beautiful, just like you. She had your wonderful red hair. I never saw a picture of her before." His face became serious and he looked at Jôn. "We must protect you, Jôn, will you be my witness?"

Jôn looked closely at Scott, "You're that serious, then? You know what you may be getting into, don't you? What does she say? Does she know her danger?"

Scott nodded, "Of course, I know, but . . ." He put both hands on each side of her cheeks and looked into her green eyes, "L'eo R'oaks, will you take me for your protector? I swear by Gaia's Universe that I will give my life for you and cherish and love you and any children we might keep for as long as our hearts shall beat."

L'ora felt his hands tremble, the intense look he was giving her and the waves of deepest feeling that rocked through her from his entire nervous system made her realize that he felt this to be something of the most crucial importance in his life.

"You must answer," Jôn directed her, rubbing his pale scalp. "Do you accept his lifetime commitment and be prepared to join him with yours?"

She stammered, "W-what should I say? Am I bonding myself to him forever? He will never leave me to be alone again?"

Jôn looked at her, "You must answer from your heart and you should know that he may be giving up his life's position to become an outlaw to protect you. He is risking his everything for you. Once this contract is filed, whatever you are accused of or condemned to, he will share your sentence."

L'ora looked into Scott's piercing blue eyes, "But I have done nothing, what is wrong about me?" She looked from one man to the other, recognizing the serious expressions on their faces. "You would do that for me, Scotty? I will put you in danger? I don't want that."

"I am already committed, L'eo, I have made my promise."

She looked at him and echoed his feelings with her own. "I, L'ora R'oaks, swear to accept your promise and by Gaia's Ever-Changing Universe, I will give you my love and honor and place any of our children under your protection as my partner and life's companion until our hearts cease to beat."

He picked her up and placed her on his lap, "Jôn, now we're united against all the foes of the Universe." His kisses relayed feelings she could never have imagined and she found herself returning them with all her heart.

"So recorded and filed," answered Jôn, then, realistically, "Now what is the cabinet number for your Bonding feast?"

L'ora slipped out of his arms and ran to the counter to peer over to the slot for the tokens and trace the number on the raised brass plaque. She ran back smiling and said, "It's easy 4-1776-1787."

The two men looked at each other. "The die is cast," Jôn said, "You know what this place is and what will happen if they find you here."

Scott nodded and drew L'ora close, looking up at Jôn's face on the wall. "We'll celebrate first and then I have something amazing that you need to read," he said. "I will hold it up for you to record and then we will decide what to do. I realize now what Silversuit Master First had been searching for during these past years and to have it fall into my hands after his death is ironic. I have some of his belongings in my cubicle to bring here. He had begun to talk about strange things and I thought when he made me promise to get his belongings, it was because he was dying. I really did not look carefully in the things he entrusted me."

Scott's expression changed and almost cheerfully he said, "For a number four for two people, how much do I owe you including the bubbly?"

Jôn said, "The condemned man and the herb of rue?" He named a price that made L'ora gasp and when Scott reached into his pouch and brought out a shiny gold coin and gave it to her, indicating for her to place it in the slot, she just stared at him.

"This is more than I make in a year and we're going to waste it on food?"

Scott smiled and waved her on, "The next one is going on clothes for you. For something as important as a Bonding Day, your rags aren't very appropriate. You will have to have your dress after and not before the event. Of course, you should have proved that you were pregnant before the ceremony but we will have to do something about that afterwards as well."

Jôn indicated the small door over the counter, "Your first course is almost there. Take your time and enjoy every bite. Once this gets going, you may never have another chance." He continued with a sad expression, "Good-bye, my friend. May the Good Mother Gaia protect you and keep you both safe." His admiring glance at L'ora was their last look at his face as the picture faded.

Chapter 9

A Break in Time

L'ora slid the small door up and lifted the platter out. "What's this?" she asked, smelling the strange stringy and unappetizing looking things she was offering to Scotty.

"They're the "legs" of a kind of sea plant," he said, "rip the leathery covering off and just eat the part inside."

That was the first of many unknown foods she withdrew from the dumb waiter and each had a taste completely different from the other. Tiny cups of lemon ice came with each course to erase the taste of one food from the next.

Scott withdrew the bottle packed in a circular container filled with blue glacier ice. He twisted off the wire net over the top, holding it down and slowly let the cork push its way until, with a small pop, it came out without spilling a drop.

He poured some in two long thin crystal goblets that arrived on the tray and offered one to her. "Jôn has sent us a Bonding gift," he told her, indicating the delicate crystal. "Now, here's to him and to us, and happiness as long as we can have it." He touched her crystal flute with his and raised it up in the air, "To our success and to those that have prepared our way."

She took a sip, blinking at the tiny drops that bubbled out like flames from a lit sparkler on Constitution Night. Her second sip was longer and she started to drink it down.

Scott laid his hand on hers, "L'eo, this is to be sipped, not drunk and since you have never had any before, you must drink it very slowly. These bottles are unique, after they finish there may never be any more. The older barren women that work the warm food producing areas have too much work to do producing food for the ice cities. They have no time to make this very special bubbly."

"My name is L'ora, not L'eo. That was my father. You even called me that in our Bonding. Why?"

He smiled at her, "I just bonded with L'eo R'oaks, Head Archivist, not with L'ora R'oaks, a beautiful woman who might be taken any moment. That's what the records will show. We're safe that way and as long as nobody sees you, we're officially a bonded childless couple that no one will investigate unless an unlikely case comes up and the adoption committee awards us an orphan to raise. I'm going to call you Lee to keep me from making the mistake of saying your name in the wrong places."

They ate slowly with small bites, her face showing her amazement of the variety of tastes and textures. When a voice came from Jôn saying they should take a break before the next course, Scott stood up. "Now we must find your Bonding Day outfit. Jôn has sent me the name of a trusted friend of his, Facil Negash, and I'm going to put him on the wallcast."

A few minutes later the smooth face of Jôn's friend came on the wall. "Jôn said you needed help in dressing a beautiful partner in suitable bonding attire. May I see the candidate?"

Scott whispered to "Lee" and she tucked a wayward curl back under her ski cap before walking in front of the CG-glass, still keeping the gossamer cloak around her and her face shyly averted. Her figure appeared in the wall as though she were physically there, Facil Negash's amazed face watching from a corner.

"Ah," said Facil, his long black fingers forming a square to frame around her as he studied her. "A true beauty." A sad look momentarily crossed his face, "As were the beautiful women of my land."

With rapid strokes, he began to sketch on a slate board. The fir collared chamois leather full-body suit with the finest tinted Vicuña long cape, and soft reindeer boots that came over her knee caused her to clap her hands in pleasure. A fur tunic in a contrasting color finished the design.

Entranced by the beauty of his creation, L'ora sighed, "It's beautiful! I've never seen anything so lovely . . . unthinkingly she burst out, "Could I have something to match to cover my hair?"

Scott, frightened, looked at Facil as the designer said, "Real hair? I cannot believe it. For the love of Gaia, let me see it this one time, and make my dreams of ancient women come true."

Realizing her mistake, L'ora grabbed Scott's arm, "What have I done, Scotty, after all these years of hiding?"

Facil waved his hands, "I am your friend. Please, please, let me see. I cannot believe that such a thing is still possible in today's twisted world."

L'ora looked at Scott who looked at Facil and then nodded. She lifted her hand and slowly slid the soft wool covering off of her head, the freed auburn tresses flowing far down her back and shoulders.

"Ahhh," Facil said, his expressive face showing his pleasure. "You're truly a dream come true. If only I could arrange such magnificence into a creation matching my designs. It would be the crowning display of my career." The designer grew serious, "She is the most beautiful secret weapon in our arsenal. Will you take her there after I have finished? --Such a pity to have to cover such loveliness. I will create some simple outfits with bonnets as hair coverings to match. With this freezing weather, it won't be hard." As his picture faded out, his admiring glance made her cheeks turn scarlet.

"That was close," Scott said, unexpected jealousy tearing at his heart. Turning back to the shining glass desktop, he circled her waist and drew her close. "You never saw any of this? What kind of workstations did you have in the archives rooms?"

She peered at the bright CG-glass covering, "I've worked with a lot of these but never saw them all in one place. Dad taught me a piece at a time in different locations around the file shelves. After he was gone, I used to search among the corridors to see if I could find more and when I did, I tried to learn how to use them on my own. They were all keyed to our family passwords,"

She pushed a stool over beside him and began to touch different parts of the CG-glass surface that lighted up at her touch. Suddenly a kind voice spoke out of the depths of the machine.

—*L'ora, my beloved daughter, you have come of age and are working on our console.*—

There was a long pause in the recording before it began again.

—*I am not registered with you so fear I am no longer part of your life and you do not know the future you are destined to take.*—

Another pause and the voice asked, —*Is the person with you of confidence or must he be erased?*—

"No, no," she said, tears in her eyes as she heard her father's voice, "he is my Bonded partner and must be included in all this machine can teach us."

—*Register his eyes and fingertips.*—

Two thin red lights erupted from the CG-glass and twin rectangular plates materialized. Scott looked into the red pinpoints of light as his hands pressed on the two plates. Blood inside his fingers rose to his skin's surface and colored waves traveled back and forth across the red spots. A mechanical voice stated,

—His eye pattern is registered.— After a pause it started reading from a list of the components of his blood, then it changed and read out a surprising diagnose of his DNA.

—This person is of Hunter ancestry, descended from the youngest brother of the Mistress, your great-great-grandmother. From that clan came the first Silversuiters.—

L'ora looked at Scotty, "We're very distant cousins!" she said in surprise. She slipped under his arms and kissed him, "We're kissing cousins!"

Scotty pulled her close but they were interrupted by a noise from the dumb waiter that attracted their attention. A package wrapped in thin violet paper and tied with multicolored ribbons slid out of the opening of the dumbwaiter and a whiff of exotic perfume wafted around the room. L'ora pulled out of his arms and ran to retrieve the package, her eyes dancing in delighted anticipation. "Don't look," she said as she carefully untied the knots in the ribbons.

He heard her gasp as, dutifully, he turned back to the multicolored lights reflected through the CG-glass and began to learn the depths of commands that she had caused to emerge from each touch.

"Now look!" she said and Scott turned to see her twirling around and around, a multicolor fine wool cape flowing out, twisting around her and her long hair wrapping itself around her face and body. Her laughter filled the room and she seemed like a child from some long ago tale of days of multitudes of presents and long-lived parents with an impossible wealth of children.

Scott stared at Lee dancing before him, her long locks framing her face and cascading around her caped body. She glowed with the brilliant colors of the silk that covered the soft chamois and her curves were outlined by the art of the master designer. She began to sing, her entire body duplicated in the wallcast and a strange music from another time flowed around the room to accompany her.

His arms reached out and then withdrew, his anguish showing in the trembling of his voice, "You are more desirable than ever, the sight of your hair tortures me, and I cannot touch you."

Lee bent down, pulling a thick strand of hair out of a long lock that curled around her breasts. Brushing it across the uncovered space she had opened in the material around her stomach, she looked into his eyes.

His hands tried to stop her as she said, "You see, I don't believe that my silver threads will disappear when I brush them with my hair." She turned toward him and, before he realized, wrapped the long strand around his neck.

"No," he said, grabbing at his neck with both hands, "You'll kill me."

L'ora used the end of the strand to pull him down and put her arms around his neck to kiss him with all the passion she had discovered during the last hours. He snatched the strands away and then felt his neck, expecting to find the silver covering gone. Amazed, he found that the long strand had not altered the silver covering in the least. "More magic, my beautiful witch?" he sighed, immersed in the unique beauty of her hair.

"No," she said as she danced against him and wrapped him within her locks, "I couldn't believe that my hair and your silver skin would clash if we loved each other. You see, it is both a defensive material and an informative one. You say it discovers lies, I think it also uncovers love."

Scott looked at her and with wary fingers reached out and slipped his hands into her long tresses. For a moment he caught his breath and then grabbed masses of her hair in both hands and buried his face in it. "I've wanted to touch and hold your hair ever since I first saw it and now you have unleashed my deepest desire." He brought her lips to his through her waves and passionately kissed her again and again. His fingers searched to open the catches in the glowing silk tunic; pulling it away from her body. He guided her toward the large frame of the bed cubicle, lifted her up, and slid her into the soft linen sheets. Following her through the open mist of the frame he said, "This is our Bonding night and we're going to make it the first of a lifetime of memorial nights. We can have the rest of the feast for breakfast."

Chapter 10

The Conclave

"Quickly! Open the frame, Mistress L'ora," the voice commanded, waking the two bodies still wrapped in sleep. They looked at each other, what had wakened them so long before dawn? They slipped out of the bed frame, L'ora trying to dress in yesterday's finery while Scott picked her up and ran to a corner, placing her behind him and standing before her in an aggressive stance. Before they could even question the voice, the wall lit up with the shadows of a caped and hooded group of men filling up the hall outside the frame. Their tall wooden staves with thin strands flowing from the knobbed tops gave a military appearance to the invading company.

"Stop!" Scott called out, showing his strong silver body in the wallcast that reflected his full-sized hologram among those in the hall.

"Scott, we need to be inside immediately," Facil Negash said, dropping the intricately woven hood away from his dark face and showing his tall thin body to the wallcast. "The men in this group are the leaders of our Constitutionalist army and we have not been able to convene since Master R'oaks was taken. Jôn has sounded the summons and we are here to confirm the news that the lost has been discovered. Do you truly have it?"

The group of shadowy men murmured in anticipation to their answer. They pressed against the frame, whispering in anxious voices.

"Let us in, don't keep us out here in suspense."

"It's dangerous for us to be here."

"We've come to see if the impossible may be true."

A bent figure was helped forward and he reached out, his soft plated arm thrusting through the frame which, obedient, misted open, letting the group rush in, the frame becoming solid behind them. Before Scott could catch her, L'ora rushed out from behind him and palmed off the alarm before the first wail started.

She whirled to look at the men that packed the large room, surprised at their reactions.

"It's the Mistress come back to lead us!"

"Great Gaia, our prayers have been answered!"

"The red hair. . . the red hair, it's uncut."

"She is beautiful like the Mistress was."

"Lovely vision; help us to free our wives and families."

"She is our beautiful secret weapon."

"It's a miracle of which only the Earth Mother is capable."

"Don't exaggerate, but there is no doubt that she is of the Mistress' blood." The bent figure with the master wrist plate stepped toward L'ora, Scott's strong figure preventing him from getting too close. His voice croaked with age, "Are you the daughter of Leonardo Robles, known as Lee R'oaks? Son of Carlos Robles, son of Manuel Robles, son of Sebastian Robles II and Eleanor Palma, youngest daughter of the Mistress and the Saviour?"

"Yes," said L'ora, clinging to Scott's arm; his strength running through her nerves. Surprised that her inquirer should know of her ancestors, she began to understand why her father and grandfather had made her learn the branches of her family tree.

The bent figure turned to Scott. "A Silversuiter here beside the inheritor of our vanished leaders? How did this amazing occurrence happen?"

"We're Bonded," said L'ora looking up at him with pride, "Scott is of the Hunter Clan and is one of us. You can check his DNA."

"Master," Scott said, bowing his head, "I was the protégée of Silversuit Master First. You must have known him as he also wore a master wrist control. But. . . you are not a Silversuiter."

"No," the ancient spokesman replied, "I am Nicolas II and was at the very birth of the Silver ones when we were helping the teachers to form armed groups and escape to save the children. Look!" He held out his wrinkled hand to show the silver tendrils that threaded across his hands and covered the faint networks of blood that coursed just under his parchment skin. "Silversuit Master First became the first true Silversuiter and we have kept in touch throughout his century." He reached out and took Scott's hand. "You have his control and that means that he is no longer with us." His face reflected his pain and he sighed, "I saw the Hero Teachers evolve into respected rulers and, as the bacteria decimated the world's population, into dictators and finally into controllers of the intellectual development of the surviving children of the world. We have been hunted down and there are few of us in any one place now as we're spread among the populated ice cities. Many of the younglings have never learned anything of real human history. The great libraries of the world remain lost in the abandoned cities in the warm areas of the world and the few undeleted information clouds are controlled directly by the very few allowed under the Master Teacher's dictates."

Scott looked through the group that milled around the room. Most of them were older with few young faces among them. "What do you want us to do?" he asked, looking at the hopeful faces before them.

"First, assure us that you actually do have a copy of the original Constitution." a younger man answered, saying the word with great veneration.

"Wait here." Scott told them. Taking Lee by the hand they walked through the doorframe and crossed the icy corridor into her tiny room. They turned to her bed frame; both thinking how cold her room was compared to the room across the hall marked "Storage."

Scott rescued the priceless booklet from the floor while L'ora picked up Cato and snuggled him into her soft wool cape. She unhooked her carrysak from the C.H.A.R. and hung it on her shoulder.

They returned to the much larger room, finding the amazed group inspecting the furnishings of the room and its complicated electronic devices, still glowing with power unlike any they had ever seen.

"Behold!" said Scott, holding up the thin book innocently covered in cheap brown paper with childish scrawls covering up the title: *Laws*. He folded back the brown paper and disclosed the original booklet where letters printed in bright red and white colors read, "**Our Constitution - 1787**."

A collected sigh spread through the group and several called out, "read it."

Scott stood up, his height enabling him to look over the group. He carefully opened the book and L'ora pointed to the CG-glass. She touched parts of the controls and indicated to Scotty to lay the book on the special glass. As he did so the images and text of the first two opened pages appeared across the wallcast with the first line in large bold letters.

With reverent tones all started reading the hallowed words:

"We the People . . . ""*We the people --- in order to form a more perfect Union, establish justice, insure domestic tranquility, provide for the common defense, promote the general welfare, and secure the blessings of liberty to ourselves and our posterity, do ordain and establish this Constitution . . ."*

Chapter 11

Plans

A dawn ribbon of Northern Lights barely showed through the blizzard's white gales and still the group of men crowded around the CG-glass frame of the control desk. The younger of the group said in despair, "There's no way we can learn all this before the end of the holiday week. We can't even fit close enough to see the controls."

Scott stood up, sliding Lee off of his lap where they had been instructing the group on the use of the advanced electronics. "You're right, and you need some rest." He palmed a corner of the glass and even L'ora was surprised to see a diagram of her part of the building from "L" corridor all the way to her "Z" corridor. The rooms showed a combination of figures in each one and he pointed to the ones in the "X" and "Y" corridors. "These "official" charts show these rooms are occupied with the normal activity of childless couples. They don't use the lifts because this sector backs against the mountain and the outside emergency corridors open onto the mountainside walkways. We must all study the diagrams so that if the Supreme Master Teacher's army ever attacks our center, we will be able to flee to the mountain. L'ora tells me that she has seen no one here for years. This indicates to me that this is part of the plan that you have been training for and that the R'oaks were the leaders. L'ora will be the figurehead of the movement as she is now of age."

He buried his face in her shoulder and said in a low voice that only she could hear, "My love, even I cannot protect you from now on although I put my life at your feet."

L'ora looked at the expectant and respectful faces around them. "What am I to do?"

Scotty looked at her, the sadness in his eyes abating.

"First we must unite all our people and prepare for the worldwide revelation. Master Nicolas, please assign these rooms to your followers and open them so all can rest. This building complex has enough rooms for quite an army but we must have communications open to your contacts throughout the world. They must know our plans before the end of this week and we must train as many as possible to enter into the secret communications network" He looked at L'ora, "From what I have found out, this is a powerful console but not the master control. It cannot break through the protected cloud information. Do you know where it is? Could it be in your grandfather's room?"

L'ora shook her head. "I don't know, we'll have to get into his room. Shall we try now?"

Scott stood up. "All please follow Master Nicolas for him to assign your rooms. You have ten hours to get anything you need from where ever you came from. The blizzard will be your protection. Console training for those staying will be starting in an hour."

Master Nicolas indicated for the group leave the room. He pointed to the golden knobs on top of their staffs. "Your staves will open your assigned door. The inventor of the binary curtain frames and the access rings and controls was one of us.

Those without staves will be given special rings. We will send word to all those who have been in hiding these five years to return to this building. "

Scott took L'ora by her hand and they walked into the hall and turned left toward the large frame marked "Maintenance." Walking up to the frame, Scott held out his control wrist to open the solid looking frame curtain. The instant his control started to pass, a huge spark and a crackle as of thunder sent him spinning to the floor.

L'ora dropped down beside him, "Scotty, Scotty, are you all right?" She felt for the pulse in his neck and, frightened, placed her hands over his sternum and pounded as hard as she could.

Just coming out of the 'Storage' frame, Master Nicolas, followed by several of his group, rushed beside her. One of them knelt beside her and repeated her movement still harder.

Scotty jerked and his eyes opened. "What was that?" he said, seeing the anxious faces around him and L'ora's tears. He tried to sit up but the one who had helped her pushed him back down.

"I'm a Medic, just be still for a while, you've had a shock that would have killed a lesser man." He looked at L'ora and pointed to the 'Maintenance' frame, "What's in there?"

"I think that's the master control room but if Scotty can't get in, I don't know how we're going to." She looked at Master Nicolas, "You have a master control, do you think it will open the frame?"

"I think there is more to that frame than a master control can open. There must be another way in. If anyone can open it, I think it will be you."

The Medic gestured to two of the men to help Scotty back into the 'Storage' room.

"Watch him, don't let him get up for a while."

"Lee, we must get into that room." Scotty said, looking at her where she sat beside him on the large C.H.A.R. "Maybe you can find the answer among the desk controls."

"I'll look, but am going to stay here now to make sure you don't get up." L'ora picked up his hand. "Did your Silverskin protect you from the shock?" She looked at the darkened skin where even the silvery shine was blackened over an angry red blister. "Does it hurt? Shall I put some of your cream on it?"

He shook his head, "Silver cream is very rare and I think we had better save what is left, we may need it for more serious wounds."

"I've thought of something. I can take some of the younger members to the archives and train them on the consoles there. The room I got into yesterday doesn't have any observation eyes anywhere; Dad said so in the birthday instructions he left me to follow. There are many consoles we can use. It seems that everything in that room is protected and the entrance frame is hidden between the long rows of multicolored wires that labyrinth the archives."

She reached into her carrysak, "Here, I forgot this," and brought out a thick book titled 'The Federalist Papers.' "I think this also has something about the Constitution times."

Chapter 12

Preparations

A week later, Scott looked at the small square on the corner of the wallcast. "Jôn, we cannot be ready in time without the master control. We need to be able to reach every working wallcast in the world at the same time and for that we have to be able to connect to and manage the secret worldwide energy cloud. Everything we have been able to fathom through this console and the ones in the archive rooms points to that."

He watched the frame open and L'ora enter with her large group of enthusiastic young console trainees, their worshipful glances at her awaking jealous pangs in his heart. "Jon, you were too right about our having our Bonding feast when we could. These days Lee and I scarcely see each other."

Jôn understood the look on Scotty's face. "We've been picking up more individual groups than we ever thought still existed. The first were 'Cheyenne', 'Nebraska', Jigokudani' and 'Penguin'. Just today,

'Baikal', 'Kiwi', 'K2' and 'DEW' came in and yesterday 'Khan', 'Edelweiss,' 'Kilimanjaro', 'Samiyax' and 'Aconcagua'. Here, look at this list."

Scott read from this list, smiling at the odd names, "Some of these are so far out of the way, they aren't even using a code name, 'Yakulsk,' 'Vostok,' 'IFalls', 'Pyongyang', 'Fraser,' 'Barrow,' 'Ruapehu,' 'Frodo,' and even our 'Sleeping Lady,' and 'Popocatepetl' . . . I don't see how anyone could be living on that active volcano even if it is covered in ice."

"The word *Federalist* is the key word set in when we first started resisting the teachers turned dictators. Each of your consoles is pinpointing different parts of the icy world with protected shoots. You're doing a great job. How close are you to getting into the master console?"

Scott shook his head, his eyes bleary from countless hours spent searching the possible routes on Lee's father's computer. When L'ora would find him dropping to sleep over the CG-glass, she would push him to the C.H.A.R and take over but neither had any luck.

He felt her welcome arms around his neck and spun around in his chair to hold her close.

"We only have 24 hours left, Scotty, what can we do? I keep feeling that the answer is right under my nose but don't know what it is."

Jôn broke in, "There's a world-wide message coming in from the Supreme Master Professor, open up your cast."

The hated Teacher's Council music blared out and the once-handsome face of the Supreme came on the wallcast. "Devoted pupils of the world, we are postponing the festivities until next weekend. The blizzard will be over by then and we can join you in a proper recognition of the incomparable Constitution." His face faded out as imaginative shots of the festivities to come shot across the wall.

"Everyone, take twelve hours off." Jôn said, "Don't think of what we're searching for, maybe your subconscious will find the answer."

Scott nodded, pulling Lee close and heading for her room across the hall "I can think of something to keep our minds off of everything," he said with a conspirators' grin. "Even your icy room looks wonderful right now."

She snuggled into his arm and they fled into her room, hardly waiting for the frame to close behind them.

L'ora woke first and slipped out of Scotty's loving arms as a 3D projected dawn approached. Cato was waiting by the cabinet and she realized that she had not fed him the day before. "I'm sorry Cato," she told him as she scraped a full portion of food into his bowl and put it on his accustomed side of the C.H.A.R. Squeezing in beside him, she pulled the old blanket over them and clicked the warming toggle. When he had finished his food, he climbed onto his accustomed place in her lap, curling up and purring while his claws made 'happy paws' pinpricks on her leg. She scratched behind his ears and rubbed a finger under his chin, pushing aside his ornate collar. "How did you get out of the 'storage' room?" she asked him lazily. "Did you go all the way around the compound?"

Her attention flew to Scotty who had slipped out of the bed frame and was stretching his body, his arms almost touching the ceiling of her small room. In two steps he was beside her, pulling her out of the C.H.A.R. and awaking her passion with his kisses.

A cold blast made Scott spin around, holding L'ora behind his back. Seeing the Silversuiter in the frame he demanded, "Herdez, what are you doing here?"

With his face turning red, his companion stammered, "I, I brought your pass back, I didn't mean to interrupt anything. You'll need it for entrance to the compound tomorrow."

A young woman stepped out from behind him, a tiny fuzz of dark hair showing through her shaved scalp.

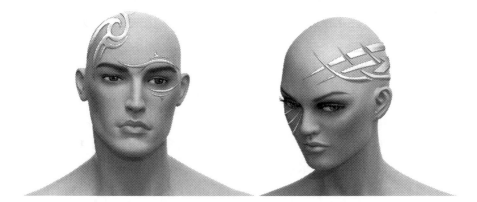

"This is Joana," Herdez said proudly, "she has conceived and we are Bonded."

L'ora stepped out from behind Scott, her long red hair waving from the chill wind blowing through the opened frame. "Welcome," she greeted Joana as both newcomers stared at her, marveling at her forbidden wealth of hair.

Scott tried to stop her as she walked toward Joana. "Lee, what are you thinking of? He must turn you in."

"No," she answered, looking deeply into Herdez's eyes. "They will be our companions, I feel their loyalty."

Herdez, trapped by her gaze, said, "What magic is this? Are you a reincarnation of the Mistress? Her picture has been handed down for generations in our family. I am named Karlos for the medic who saved her life."

"You have much to learn about what is happening," L'ora said, still holding his eyes with hers as she held out her hand to Joana. "Come with us."

Amazed, Scott watched Herdez follow her with Joana walking behind them. He shadowed them as they crossed to the frame and reached over their heads to activate their entrance.

As a group they walked into the room, attracting curious glances from the people back from their break.

L'ora pointed to the wallcast where all the pages of her pamphlet were constantly displayed when no one was sending or receiving from the console. "Read that," she told them, "and come back to us afterwards."

Scott looked at her, "How did you know that he would not follow the Silversuit rules and turn you in to the Master Teachers?"

"Because I realize that it was no accident that you were sent to me and I think that Herdez is also part of a plan whose author we do not know. His DNA will show if I am right."

As Karlos started reading the wallcast, Joana turned to them and asked, "Are you Bonded?"

Before Scott could say anything L'ora stepped in front of him. "No." she said.

When Herdez and Joana were out of earshot, Scotty looked at her in anger, "Why did you say that?"

"You bonded with L'eo R'oaks, remember?" she replied but could say no more as a group of her trainees came up to ask her to help them with a problem on one of the portable consoles that had been found among the electronic treasures in the room. She looked at him, "Don't worry, I'll explain tonight."

Leaving Scott with a distraught face, she squeezed his hand and followed the students toward the U-shaped lunch table that was being used with the tiny consoles.

Much later she came over to where he was showing another group the controls of her father's electronics. He pulled her to him and gestured to his pupils to leave. "Now tell me what you meant when you said that we were not Bonded. You can't just put me aside like that."

"No, Scotty my love, I will never put you aside. However we do have a way of protecting each other if one of us is captured. If we are asked if we are Bonded, we can truthfully say no, and what makes it true is that we Bonded 'as long as our hearts shall beat' and your heart stopped beating. Then if I am captured, you are no longer responsible for me."

Scotty looked desperate, "Those young trainees of yours, one has captured your feelings. I can't bear to think of that." He raised his fist to strike the nearest table but she ran under his arm.

"No, Scotty. Please don't think my feelings for you have changed. When this is over, we can have the most elegant Bonding ceremony you could wish for. But now, if we are interrogated, we can honestly protect each other by saying we are not Bonded. Remember, I need to carry your child to make it a true Bonding." She took a quick look at Joana and Karlos and then took both his hands, "We have a technical loop-hold, but our spiritual bond is as strong as ever." She touched the lower part of her stomach, "My silver threads assure me that we will have a child that will be the founder of a new bloodline, one resistant to the bacteria. My father's archives have shown me that great planning has gone into my family's breeding and they have been looking for the combination that will make mankind resistant to this pestilence. The curse will no longer kill families. But, we must first make the bastions of humanity free of this dictatorship."

Chapter 13

Capture

Arms entwined, Joana and L'ora watched the two Silversuiters march out the portal toward the lifts. L'ora turned to face her new friend. "You don't know how wonderful it is for me to have you to talk to. I've never had a woman friend. Dad always kept me apart from any other families because he was afraid someone might see my hair. Great-great-gran made us promise that it would never be cut."

Joana touched the long waves. "It seems selfish but one of my personal wishes about us getting rid of the dictators is that I can grow my hair long like yours."

L'ora laughed, but then grew pensive, "Do you think Roland and Robert will accept Scotty into the guards for the Master Teacher's Lounge?"

"Karlos says that they've been searching for new Silversuiters, there has been so few new young men accepted by the silver threads that they are worried about the future. They want those pairs that will not want to touch the Tenured Teachers." She looked at the dark circles under L'ora's eyes and changed the subject. "Which console do you want me to manage? I've had a lot of practice running the main console at my old Treeline Community."

"Can you? That's wonderful. Please take my group of young wannabes. Be sure to tell them you're Bonded and that you and Karlos are expecting. Scotty is turning green watching the way they try to impress me and then he gets angry. I suppose that they are all around my age but I feel hundreds of years older and that I'm babysitting them."

Joana laughed. "I'll tell Karlos that I've taken them off your back so he can tell Scott." She watched L'ora put one of her new heavy capes over Scotty's gossamer cloak and fasten the puffy Scottish design bonnet that concealed her hair "Are you going out alone? That bunch of youths always hanging around you are pests but it's safer having them underfoot than going out alone. Why don't you take some of the older men?"

"I'm OK, don't worry, I've been taking the same route since I was ten."

Joana looked worried, "But you weren't a beautiful woman then and you aren't wearing rags today."

L'ora just smiled and walked through the misty frame. "I'll be back for lunch, I just had a new hunch of which console to look for clues."

"Drat!" L'ora exclaimed early that afternoon as she left the huge archives building, *I thought I had something but that old console only kept asking the answers to children's riddles.*

The heavy sleet had changed to a light snow so she knew the celebrations would start that weekend. *So little time.* As she walked toward the pod station, the pieces of the ancient nursery rhyme kept running through her head. *Saint Ives, now who was going to Saint Ives? And where is Saint Ives? . . . It was about a person who met someone with seven wives and they were all carrying sacks.* The words began to come back to her and she skipped a step or two as she began to remember more of the rhyme the console repeated. *It's a riddle.*

As she passed a thick hedge, a ragged man with a broom suddenly accosted her. "Well now, lad, how come no one's brought you in yet? You'll bring a good number of marks. The Supreme says all young men must come to the Brain Palace." He grabbed her arm and pulled her toward him.

L'ora whirled and punched him hard on the ribs. She pulled from his loosened grip, ducked around him, and sprinted for the pod station. An earsplitting whistle rang out behind her as she reached the bottom steps. Taking the steps in leaps, she reached the platform and ran toward the transport pod. *Good, it's just preparing to pull out, I've got to make it before he catches me.*

She raced by one of the station's thick supporting pillars, concentrating on reaching the last pod.

L'ora never saw her danger until her arms were grabbed from each side by two men who jumped out from behind the pillar. The first man caught up with them as she pulled one arm free and began raining blows on the two surprised men. He threw his arm around her neck from behind and began squeezing her throat to stop her shouts for help.

"Let go of me!" She pulled at the hands around her throat as she kicked and fought, gasping for breath until she began to falter. The two grabbed her kicking legs and pushed them into a sack. The other threw a smelly sack over her head and shoulders and stout arms held her tightly. The pressure on her neck eased, allowing the sack to be tied around her throat.

With all her remaining strength she screamed, "Scotty, help!"

The three men wrapped more restraining cords around the sacks that bound her until she could scarcely wiggle. They picked her bound body up and started for the pod station.

A commanding voice just behind them shouted, "Let him go!" She felt a quiver run through her captor, causing him to let go of his end of the bundle. L'ora fell sideways from his arms and hit the stone floor with a sickening thud. His fellow cronies gave one look at the Silversuiter holding their leader, dropped her feet and turned to run, dashing into the pod as it prepared to float out of the station.

"What do you think you're doing?" The bounty collector faced the angry Silversuiter. "I have direct commands to bring in any young people who have escaped the searches and I had a tip there were some around this station. The Supreme Master is desperate and is even asking for apprentices to be brought in to fill the needs of the Council." He looked down at the limp figure in the ragged sacks. "You better not have killed this one, he's the most beautiful lad I've ever seen and will bring me a fortune in the auction."

Silversuiter Fifty knelt down and felt the throat of the unconscious figure through the sack. "Don't worry, he's got a strong pulse." He picked up the light figure and started for his nearby police pod. "You, what's your name?"

"Gulliver." the bounty hunter muttered and followed Fifty's indication to climb behind the front seat of the two-seater patrol pod.

Fifty climbed into the control seat, still holding the bundle in the sacks. He held it up as the protective belts fastened around him. Punching twice made a longer belt fasten his captive against him. A spoken command and the pod rocketed up and aimed at the complex glowing on a distant mountainside.

As the pod raced through the air, Fifty wondered, *Did I really hear a cry for help?* He felt the figure inside his arms begin to stir and a faint moan sounded through the burlap sack.

The outlines of the immense gilded Brain Palace came closer and the bound figure began to strain with gathering strength against the protective straps.

A horrible smell was the first thing L'ora realized through the waves of pain that throbbed in her mind. She opened her eyes and could see a faint light though the coarse burlap that scratched her cheeks.

The rough cloth rubbed against her arms and between the wide belt that tightly bound her against a warm body.

An arm reached through the space between the two sacks and brushed her arm as it felt for her pulse. Feeling the control on her captor's wrist, L'ora sighed, "Great Mother Gaia, Scotty, you heard me." She freed a hand from under the controlling strap, and slid it out through the space to reach and encircle the neck of the Silversuiter who held her. "Can you take this smelly cloth off or are you hiding me with it?"

Fifty felt her fingers touch his skin as her hand circled his neck. His entire body was electrified as waves of love swept over it and an overwhelming desire to be kissed and loved shocked him. The powerful force from the unknown lad's fingers flowed through his synapses, awaking sensuous desires.

Unfamiliar thoughts raced to her mind and L'ora, shocked, pulled her fingers back as if burned. "Where are you taking me? She said as she felt the pod scraping on cement and stopping,

A cold wind blew into the opening pod and strong arms held her as the straps disappeared from around them. L'ora started to struggle as she felt the seat they were on spin sideways and her captor stand up to carry her out of the pod. She struggled harder but other hands held her tightly as he straightened up.

She heard a whisper in her ear, "Strange lad, who are you? How is it possible that you not responding to my Silversuit inquiries?"

"Who are *you* and where are we?" she replied to the unknown Silversuiter, as she projected her own mental probe.

Chapter 14

The Council Chamber

The Silversuiter's arms held her tightly as a door whistled behind them and she heard the voice that accosted her say, "You don't have to carry him, just put him on the seat beside you. This fancy pod's not going to bump him around."

An unfamiliar voice said, "He's too strong for me to let loose." L'ora felt it was the voice of the Silversuiter who had whispered in her ear. His arms were still holding her close. "I'm Fifty," he managed to whisper into her ear. 'Who are you?"

L'ora didn't answer and remained silent as the pod raced up at a steep angle and finally docked smoothly. Fifty stepped out and she heard the footsteps of another person beside him. A snap of arms being presented and a commanding voice asked for identification. The Silversuiter replied and then they were out of the cold and walking down a long corridor, their feet making no noise. She thought of a thick carpet and wondered where they were taking her. Another snap of arms and they paused before walking into a warm area where many voices silenced their discussions.

A voice she had heard all her life said, "Strap him on the interrogation wall."

Strong hands pushed her against a wooden frame and her tunic was pulled up so a wide strap could be fastened around her waist and buckled tight over her leather skinsuit. Wide hooks were pulled down over her shoulders and her arms were stretched out and strapped on two long unmovable wooden paddles fixed to the wall.

The voice of the Supreme Master Teacher rang out again across the room. "All right, Comrades, let's see if Gulliver has brought a lad as beautiful as he promised."

Her legs were lifted up as the burlap was pulled off and she found herself placed against a thin wooden ledge only barely wide enough to half support her. Her swift kick sent one of those binding her rolling backwards and she heard a crash as he hit something hard. Riotous male laughter followed her blow.

"A feisty one," someone said, "good on you, Gulliver."

"Now," she heard the voice of her assailant, now identified as Gulliver. "This is your first sight before we start the bidding. You can see these are part of a young lad so only those of you interested will be bidding. As the bidding rises, we will show you the rest unless some one reaches a top price before we uncover all. Now, who wants to start with a bid of five gold marks?"

L'ora heard several male voices crying out higher and higher bids as she was pulled about and her coat and loose over-clothes were opened up; showing her fine leather body suit and her long fur tunic. Scotty's gossamer cloak was still covering her as the top sack was rolled up to her chin.

The bidding grew faster as many voices yelled amounts that made her murmur, "I *can't* be worth that much, who could have so many credits?"

Voices shouted out, "The face, let us see his face." The bidding slowed as the sack was pressed against her face and the voices said, "We can see he's young, but is he pretty or are you hiding some defects?"

"Who's going to pay to unveil his face?"

Shouts offered higher sums and then were silenced by a familiar commanding voice; "One thousand gold marks!" She felt the guards beside her step back as the room fell silent.

The footsteps approached and trembling hands lifted the sack from her head and she looked into the eyes of the Supreme Master Professor. His lecherous expression had nothing to do with the public image always portrayed on the wallcast. He reached up with wrinkled claws and placed his hands on her cheeks, holding her as he kissed her.

Behind him his personal Silversuit guard stood at attention, his face reflecting his distaste at his sworn commander's actions.

The once impressive leader pulled the edge of the tightly fastened strap around her head and dragged off her wool bonnet.

Shocked cries rang out over the room and excited shouts broke out:

"He's a woman!"

"Hair, she has hair!"

"Where could she have come from?"

"Great Gaia, she's beautiful."

"It's the Mistress!"

"Whoever bonds with her will rule."

"Find out if she's Bonded."

"If she's of age, she can be interrogated."

Supreme's voice stilled all comments, "Her hair is red, and she looks like the Mistress. She *is* the long awaited leader of the people's legends."

He kept feeling her hair and rubbing his hands on her body. "She must be tested. If her DNA is of the Mistress and Saviour's lines, she is to be confined to my quarters. Bring the medical inspectors."

He looked at her and told his personal Silversuiter guard, "Here, Third, hold her hand, I must interrogate her, and you must tell me if she speaks the truth.

Third took her hand; pulling her wrist through the metal cuff as far as her arm would go until it filled the cuff and her elbow was painfully pressed into the metal manacle. The one she knew as Fifty did the same with her other arm. Stepping away from her body, Third gave a curt nod to the Supreme Master Professor.

"How old are you?" Was the first question and she gave him the same answer she had given Scott over three weeks before.

He smiled at the fascinated group of men that had left their chairs around the conference table and pressed close to watch the questioning.

"Are you Bonded?" he asked again and she paused a long time before answering. "Answer me, you know what Bonding means, don't you? You are paired with a man until his heart stops beating. Has a man caused you to be gravid so that you can Bond?" His hands kept touching her and she shrank from the pinching and rubbing he was giving her.

"N-no." she answered, and felt a pull on her hand and looked desperately at the Silversuiter who held it.

The Professor turned to the head Silversuiter, "Has she told the truth, Third?"

The head Silversuiter paused before answering. "She is very confused, Master, I have never felt such emotion from a captive. Apparently she is telling the truth." He looked at Fifty who nodded.

"Good. Then I can keep her as my captive until she bears my child. She will stand beside me and we will truly become the legendary leaders of the world. If she does not obey, we can send her to the Consequentors to force her until she is able to repent and have my child." He seemed to smile and waived to the men who were coming in through the door with medical crosses on their uniforms. "Medic Mancera, check out this woman."

The head of the medical group looked at the body of the young woman before him as he pulled his medbox from his belt. He spent a time feeling her body, then, with an evil smile, he pressed the box against her leather body-skin and over her from head to toe. Finishing his examination, he pushed it against her bare hand with force, making a few drops of blood spill from the machine. "This test will be ready in an hour, after we will take her to repeat the testing with more advanced machines to make sure everything is correct. She seems healthy but very thin and shows malnutrition." Mancera's narrow eyes looked at her and he again felt around her ribs and pinched her cheek.

The Supreme looked at him with burning eyes, "You can't have her, she is mine. Touch her again and you will be banished to the hot fields to work under the farm women until the bacteria gets you."

The men around her smiled and an audacious one said, "If she doesn't take, can we have turns to see if one of us is the lucky one?"

The Supreme One turned on him, "GET OUT! All of you, leave; NOW. I require quiet and time to begin."

The group looked at each other and at her with envious and lewd looks, and a few whispered, "He's far too old."

"He's trying to prove he's still young."

"He's knows he's losing his power."

"He thinks she will make him seem young again."

The room cleared swiftly; the last ones turning envious and mocking looks over their shoulders

Supreme held out a clinking bag before greedy Gulliver's eyes. Then he struck him sharply across the back with a shiny object from his belt. "Your shoulder blade has been tagged. If you ever mention what you have seen in this room, you will suffer terribly before your death."

Gulliver snatched the heavy bag and ran out of the room.

Chapter 15

The Supreme Lecher

L'ora looked at the three men left, the two Silversuiters stepping away from her but never taking their eyes from hers.

"Bring the interrogation consoles from my quarters, everything must recorded in here," Supreme ordered the Silversuiters and they crossed their arms in salute and marched toward the far rooms to do as they were ordered.

"Now my lovely, you *will* be the mate of the Supreme Master Professor. You must stand beside me and the world will be at our feet! We will show you can have my child and we will have the most elaborate Bonding Ceremony ever seen."

He reached for her and she pulled as far away from his grasp as possible, turning her face aside. "You cannot resist me, you have to help me, hold me and kiss me so that we can proceed with the seeding. I will send you to the Consequentors when I am finished with you if you do not join with me." He again tried to kiss her and when she did not respond, he slapped her hard.

She closed her eyes and shouted, "Scotty, I'm in the council room with the Supreme lecher."

He rubbed his ears where her scream had buried into his brain and then slapped her again and pressed his body against her. "Who is this Scotty? I'll have the Consequentors on him."

The guards returned, carrying the recording consoles with their special bases. They put them down, looking at her with wondering eyes as Fifty rubbed his ears.

The Supreme One unfastened her as he gestured to both of his guards to hold each arm while he adjusted and changed the wall structure into a thick wooden X that materialized out of the wall. They held her wrists spread wide and pulled them up, attaching them on the top parts of the X with thick leather straps. Fifty then held her struggling ankles until they could also be fastened open on the legs of the X. The silver ones kept looking at each other as they did so.

L'ora's head barely rested on a circular pad in the middle of the X-shaped padded and sheeted rack.

The Supreme dropped his robes and leaned against her, one hand starting to roll the waist of her skintight body suit down. He looked at her and stretched up for his kisses to cover her face and mouth. He never noticed what the amazed guards saw; the silver tree glowing across her stomach and they felt what she was projecting through their hands as she looked from side to side into each of their eyes.

The Supreme stood in between the bottom parts of the X-frame and pulled at her body before moving forward to rub against her. "Ah!" he said, "Your beauty is such it would awake an ancient mummy. You will bear my child and be my Bonded partner."

L'ora struggled against her restraints, making her captor laugh as he felt his beautiful captive's frantic movements against him. She became still as her fingers grasped the wrists of the Silversuiters and she closed her eyes, her projections causing unknown tremors to rock their bodies.

Supremes' motions became more ardent, "Wake me up, you witch and respond to your leader." He shook her shoulders and reached behind her waist, pulling her against him as his voice shrieked insane commands for her to make his body react to hers. He grasped her throat with one hand, pushing her head against the thin cushion, "I'll kill you if you don't wake me. Move . . .it's your fault I'm not responding."

He looked up at the Silversuiters, "Call for the Consequentors, they will make her react . . . What's the matter with you, why are you looking at me like that? Go away, leave me with her and the Consequentors." He threw himself against her again, holding his body against hers as his hand squeezed her throat.

"Stop!" Third shouted, shocking the Supreme.

"You dare talk to me that way! I'll have you banished." The angry ruler turned to them, "What could possibly make you act so insanely?"

The guards reached out and placed their hands where Third had touched her bared stomach.

Third started to unfasten her arms, "She is a Silversuiter, the first woman ever to be accepted by the silver threads. The legends say that the Mistresses' last words were that her heir, the most unique Silversuiter, had been born to lead us. She must be the one and is somehow in contact with another one of us. You cannot have her. Our oaths of loyalty now belong to her."

Third put his hand on the Supremes' shoulder and guided him away from her; the shocked leader following the commands of silver nerves forcing his hand into the metal wall cuff while the other hand snapped it closed.

Fifty said, "I couldn't be sure then but now I know that I did "hear" her call for help and when I held her in the sack, she mistook me for another Silversuiter. She has been with him and I felt a deep love. If he is still alive, we must find him."

The two strong guards unfastened her legs and helped her stand, "Come, we must go."

They gathered her clothes as she pulled her bodysuit over her waist and swiftly they left the room, the Supreme shouting after them from where he had been placed in the wall restraints that had recently been her bonds.

They closed the ornate door, making sure that his special signal that no one should enter was in its slot.

"Where is the Teacher's Lounge?" L'ora spoke for the first time, "Fourth must be there."

Third looked at her and they turned down a side hall and rushed around a corner, L'ora pulling on her outer clothes as quickly as she could.

"Wait," she said as she wrapped herself in Scotty's cape and covered her outfit by fastening on the full-length tan cape. She needed both hands to hide her tell-tale hair under the plaid bonnet and said, "You can't march me around with my hair showing."

They turned down a long corridor toward a large door guarded by two strong Silversuiters, the shorter one looking in surprise as he recognized L'ora.

"Another one for the Teacher's Lounge," Third said, returning their salute. "We were told that Silversuiter Karlos Herdez here would know what to do with her.

They were admitted just as alarm bells beeped on the Silversuiters' belts.

"What's happening?" the other guard said as he started toward them. Third reached out and grasped his plated arm as Herdez stepped forward and grabbed his companion's other hand.

The guard looked at L'ora and Third sent reassuring signals to him as Herdez said, "Yes, it is the awaited one, the great-great-granddaughter of the Mistress come to help us."

Together the small group went into the now unguarded compound. Herdez reached for L'ora's hand and indicated a passageway on the left side of the huge room they entered. "I'll check out from my shift and go with you, my companion will stay on guard."

"Scott's over there," Herdez pointed to a raised glassed room that looked over the entrances to several rooms that fanned off of the large vacant area they had just entered.

L'ora pulled out of Karlos' hand and ran up the steps to the guards' lookout center. A few seconds later she came out to the top of the stairway, "It's empty," she said.

Chapter 16

The Search

Scott had to wait until his new superior had left the guardroom before he could open the controls in the guard's console. His fingers flew over the glass panel and he keyed the secret double code for the "Storage" room. Joana answered, and he desperately asked, "Where's L'ora?" . . . "She was to have returned at lunch time?" . . . "No one knows where she could be?"

He shocked them by saying, "I '*heard*' a scream for help about an hour ago."

His fingers opened a master control with the names of the entire city's Silversuiters and their locations. He immediately saw the silver trail that led from the pod station nearest the archives straight to the building where he was now guard. "I think she's here in the Master Brain Palace! Joana, get in touch with Karlos, tell him that L'ora's in the palace and to help me find her!"

Avoiding the main door, he raced through the special opening for the guards and took the narrow passageway toward the main council room. Stopping for a minute, he concentrated, mentally searching for her thoughts to "hear" her again. A shout in his brain rocked him and he headed to the council room from where he had *'heard'* her vibrating call. Reaching the secret door that only the guards could use in an emergency, he paused a second to knock but the shouts of the Supreme erased the need for protocol and he rushed into the room and up to the bound Supreme Master Teacher.

"Sir, who did this?" --He looked at the fallen tunic and restrained himself from choking the man in front of him.

Furious, the Supreme yelled, "Don't you recognize me? Get me out of these bonds! The release catches will respond to your Silversuiter controls."

Scott felt the belt that held the partly clad leader and it opened smoothly at his touch. He opened the hand restraints that held the wrinkled and sagging arms and helped the elderly man into a chair.

"Sound the alarms!" the Supreme told him but stopped him before Scott pressed the control on his wrist. "Wait, . . . no one must know of this. Just call the guards at the main Lounge's door. I cannot let the council know what my own guards did to me."

He looked at Scott, "Have I seen you before? Are you new?"

"Sir, I have taken Silversuit Master First's place." Scott replied, "He was my mentor and was killed in an avalanche. I am called Fourth."

"Good, you can't have been around long, you are now my personal Guard. You have First's master control?" He took Scott's arm and checked the control on his wrist.

Scott looked at the aged man whose crinkled face and sagging skin belied the made-up face seen in the wallcasts and again felt anger pouring over him,

"Sir, what has happened here, why were you bound?"

"It was the witchery of a Palmer rebel, she has bewitched two of my guards and they fled with her. She must be found and brought to me and they must be eliminated."

Scott tried not to show his relief. "Yes sir, where shall we search first?"

"You must be absolutely discrete, I have to give my speech to re-open the festivities this evening and we can let nothing of this become known. I will send commands that all Silversuiters are to remain in their quarters until further notice. When the speech is over, we will have the entire city searched. Now you must go to the quarters and interrogate each Silversuiter with your master control to find out if there is any more treason among them or if anyone has ever seen her. Warn the innocent ones to be careful and let them out of the compound in pairs so that each protects and guards the other. Now find me two trusted Silver ones and hurry to search the occupants of the compound."

"Yes Sir," Scott replied, already toggling his command buttons as he rushed out of the main door of the council room. "Karlos, where are you?"

The quick answer relieved him, . . ."She's with you?"

. . . "She's all right?" . . . "She thinks she knows how to get through the other frame?" . . . "You can trust them? . . .Then go with them in a silverpod directly to the back of her residential compound and use the outside emergency walkway to enter the back of her cubicle. I need two Silversuiters loyal to us to guard the Supreme Leader." . . . "You've got a group already? Send me two, no, I'll need four and then I'll meet you at Lee's outside walkway."

He was running down the hall when he met the four Silversuiters who saluted him and awaited orders. "You know what has happened?" He touched their controls as he queried each one. Their mental reverence of L'ora revealed their total loyalty to her. "You two," he said to the ones with the highest rank, "run to the Supreme and make sure that he will be able to give his speech. Do you understand what we are planning?" Seeing their solemn nods, he turned to the other two. "Go to our compound, talk to a few at a time and prepare them for the evening's disclosure."

As he turned he saw a medical team head toward the Chambers, a tall, thin medic with narrow eyes leading them.

Chapter 17

Cato's Door

Scott ran to the Brain Palace's Silverfleet base and chose the fastest of the small patrol pods that were always ready for emergencies. He waved his wrist over the pods' control and saluted the control tower that immediately released the pod to shoot out and turn toward L'ora's compound.

Time seemed to have been instantaneous and forever until he slid into the snow on the mountain behind her huge residential complex. Climbing onto the emergency walkway, he raced around the building and spied the group just entering the back of her cubicle. Catching up with them he swept L'ora into his arms. "Lee, I thought I'd lost you! Don't ever go out unprotected again!

"Scotty, I could only think that I would never see you again!" Her feelings matched his and relief flooded both of them.

L'ora caught her breath after his hug and said, "Look, Scotty, I think the nursery rhyme the old computer has been playing may be the secret. I thought about it when I woke up in that smelly sack. What was in the sacks the wives were carrying?"

Everyone looked at her in bewilderment. Sacks? Wives? They stared at her as she chanted the ancient riddle.

"As I was going to St. Ives,
I met a man with seven wives.
And every wife had seven sacks
And every sack had seven cats.
And every cat had seven kits.
Kits, cats, sacks and wives,
How many were going to St. Ives?"

Only Scott responded although not the correct answer of the riddle, "Cats!"

Scotty grabbed her hand as she ran into her cubicle and to her C.H.A.R. She pulled off the warm throw that now covered Cato and picked him up. Rubbing behind his ears and under his chin she showed them the collar around his neck. "Dad placed this collar on him just before he disappeared. Cato has always been able to go all over but I thought it was because the collar was programed for emergency doors. When I think about it, I realize he was getting into Dad's room but I never saw him come through the corridor frame. It might put Cato in danger for us to experiment with him but we must try."

They ran across the corridor and Scott opened the 'Storage' frame before them. L'ora talked to Cato and rubbed her cheek against his. Then she carefully put him down before the empty part of the wall that separated the two rooms.

Cato looked at her and marched toward the wall, stopping before the space behind one of the consoles and sniffing its support. Then he sat down and began vigorously washing his face, ignoring the anxious looks directed at him.

"No, no, Cato, don't play cat now, please just go on through the door if there is one." She walked toward the wall with a determined step as if she was going to walk right through the wall. Cato stood up and walked beside her but he *did* walk right on through the seemingly very solid wall as she came up to it and had to stop.

"Cato, where are you? . . . Come back. . . . Here Kitty, Kitty, Kitty . . . I have some of your treats." She gestured to Scotty who quickly got the container of treats she had just been able to afford for Cato. She shook the container and the treats rattled inside it. "Here, Kitty, Kitty," she called again as she shook the treats.

Cato appeared from behind the console table and meandered over to where she was opening the container. "Here Kitty, you have earned them," and she poured all the small fish-shaped treats onto the rug. As he started crunching them, she unbuckled his collar and fixed it on her wrist. Then she walked toward the wall that disappeared before her, displaying a much larger room with electronic equipment covering every space available.

The ominous voice that greeted them said,
—If you are the heiress, look into the plate, if not, do not under any circumstance step into this room . . . your death will be your own responsibility.—

L'ora drew in her breath and bravely stepped into the room. She turned to look into the twin red lights that penetrated her eyes.

The voice said, —*Passage granted.*—

—If you are planning to set into action the Master Plan . . . the central controls are setting up to project the yearly worldwide speech by the Supreme Master Professor. If you wish to intervene, you must be swift. Forewarnings must be sent to all the squadron rooms in this compound and advisories sent to all the human residents left in the world. Four years and 24 days ago the R'oaks team left instructions that the new Mistress might appear and would need to speak to the planet.—

Scott and Karlos ran to the largest wallcast. The electronic desk before it extended across the wall and they realized that they were standing before the strongest master control on the entire planet. Here they would be able to penetrate and control the cloud so long under the control of the master computers in the Brain Palace.

L'ora started after them but Facil Negash came in with the large group of Constitutionalists that were pouring through the 'Supplies' wall frame and held her back.

"Come Joana, help me," he said to her friend who was just entering, "she must be prepared for tonight and I will get my wish to add a magnificent hair arrangement to go with her costume."

Chapter 18

The Speech

L'ora looked at the reflection in the wallcast of her cubicle. *That can't be me; I never looked like this.* She touched the multitude of small braids that interwove across the top of her head making an intricate living tiara. The rest of her long hair wove down around her body, somehow blending with Negash's beautiful fabrics. Using ancient cosmetics, he had enhanced her beauty, her green eyes seeming to glow from the heightened shades and black lines around them.

Scotty took her hand, still staring at her, "He's made your beauty a work of art, you don't just look beautiful, you look . . . regal!" He covered her hands with his. "Lee, . . . your fingers are trembling."

"Oh, Scotty, how can I do this? . . . In front of the whole world? I'm only an archivist; I've never trained to make speeches. What shall I do? . . . I feel faint. Stay beside me."

"Of course, I'll be on one side and Third on the other. But you will be the one up on the platform and trust me, you can do it."

He helped her up on the small platform they had fabricated in her cubicle against one of Negash's beautiful mixed blues fabrics. The lighting made her stand out and the flowing cape and high collar reflected her face and her long strands of hair wrapped close to her body suit.

They counted the minutes until the Supreme Master Professor's face came on the wallcast and he started his speech with a surprising statement: "People of the world, we have wonderful news; the heir of the Mistress has appeared and she is carrying my child. We will be the inheritors of the Mistress and the Saviour and make the world return to its place as it was *Before*." He held up a large medical sheet titled 'Blood work of Heiress.' Large blue letters were stamped over the other medical notes: WITH CHILD.

Scott yelled, "Cut him out, switch to Lee!"

L'ora saw the red light that meant she was live on the wallcasts of the world but she did not follow her memorized speech. Anger and fury burnt through her at the Supremes' speech and she stood straight and burst out, "I am L'ora R'oaks, great-great-grandchild of the Mistress and *I* am her designated heiress. My child is assuredly not by that decrepit liar you just saw. Next week you will be entertained by my official Bonding ceremony with its father who is my life's partner and my remote kinsman."

She paused and continued with her original speech. "I do bring hope to the world. My family has spent these generations trying to protect humanity from the bacteria and I am the living example that they have succeeded. We will publish their research as proof. You all know that the silver threads guard from the bacteria and greatly prolong the life of the Silversuiters that are selected to carry them. Look! -- I am the first female Silversuiter and the vaccines from my blood will protect the entire world's population." She opened the long rhombus in her body suit and a close-up of her skin showed the lacy silver tree that branched across her stomach and waist. "My child will be the first of a new generation of humans; all protected against the bacteria that has plagued humanity."

"Men and women of the world, no longer do you need to shave your heads. We will become partners with the Silversuiters and as such, they will not be our inquisitors but our protectors. We were not told that our hair protected us from their control of our bodies and that was the reason we were required to keep our heads shaven. As you can see, the Mistress required that I not cut my hair and those Silversuiters who are my followers are not affected when my hair touches them. Let your hair grow!" She indicated the shadowy silver figures on each side of her podium and the world could see she was not afraid of them.

"Now listen to the most important happening in our generation! The original words of the famous Constitution have been found. They are being portrayed on every wallcast in the world and will be the rules by which our societies will become free again. Read them with care and elect your own rulers to bond the world together for our new children. Read them now with me:"

Voices from the entire world joined with a reverent chorus;

"We the people --- in order to form a more perfect Union, establish justice, insure domestic tranquility, provide for the common defense, promote the general welfare, and secure the blessings of liberty to ourselves and our posterity, do ordain and establish this Constitution . . ."

Her closing "thank you" was hardly heard as the decimated populations read the words translated into their languages that would unite them and would set them free from the dictatorship of the Supreme Teachers and their control of the education of their children.

She turned from her perch and Scott caught her as she collapsed into his arms. He carried her to the C.H.A.R. and laid her gently beside Cato. "Your medical report said that you were underweight and anemic. When *was* the last time you ate?"

She opened her eyes, "I, I don't remember, didn't we have a sandwich together? . . . Scotty, could you get me a cup of hot chocolatl with real milk?"

He looked at her and laughed. "It's just what you need but when did you ever drink such an exotic and expensive drink?"

She smiled back, "At Great-Great-Gran's, they had cows and huge storehouses behind their stone walls and I've always wanted another cup."

Her new friends pressed around her, congratulating her on her speech and the multitude of responses that were pouring into the wallcasts, no longer controlled by the Brain Palace.

"The entire world is writing you, you have brought hope to those that had lost any thought of rebuilding the world." Joana told her, patting her hand. "Now you must rest, the world is responding, you can do no more today. We will help Scotty care for you and build up your strength so you can have the ceremony you promised in your speech." She turned to the packed room, "Please, leave Mistress Lee, she needs to rest as do all of us. Return to your rooms and rest, tomorrow we will start to help form the new world order."

The doctor who had resuscitated Scotty reached into his Medisak and began examining her. "Joana's right, rest and nutrients are what Mistress Lee needs right now."

As the group started to leave, each stopped by and touched L'ora's hand or bowed to her, murmuring their thanks before walking out. Negash was one of the last; he bowed to her and kissed her hand, "Goodbye, my empress, you have made me the most ecstatic of men in this sad world. I will have the hologram of you speaking on the wallcast in my office for always. Tomorrow I will start to design the most unique and beautiful Bonding dress ever."

Scotty returned with the steaming cup, "Jôn is designing special dishes to bring your strength back. He has stayed at his post to keep the confidence the teachers have in him as head of food requirements across the world. He calls this *hot chocolate*."

L'ora sipped the drink, feeling its warmth spread through her body. "It's as wonderful as I remembered, thank him for me."

Joana and Karlos were the last to slip out, leaving L'ora nestled in Scotty's warm arms. "Did you truly mean it about showing the world our Bonding Ceremony?" he whispered into her ear.

"Of course, now we can make it complete and legal." She placed his hand on her silver threaded skin. "This is your child I am carrying."

Scott shook his head as if he had not realized what her condition meant. "Feel my happiness," he said, looking into her eyes and projecting his deepest feelings. "You know how much I love you."

L'ora dozed against his chest then fell into a deep sleep.

Wonderful smells invaded her dreams and she woke to see Scotty placing a full platter between them.

"I told Jôn that we had had only a rushed breakfast this morning and that we really had not had time to eat regularly for weeks. He said for us to eat slowly and he would give us the proper food to return your strength. Eat this and enjoy it, I'll join you. Here's a pot of chocolate for both of us."

The wonderful tastes of unknown fresh fruits and vegetables and servings of real meat kept them making excited comments for the next half hour.

"Scotty, what's this" L'ora repeated for the tenth time, holding another new fruit up on her fork. "Some of the fruit in the skin is changing to sugar."

"I didn't know either and had to ask Jôn. He said it was a fruit from the *chicle* tree in the jungles where the ancient Maya lived and where something called chewing gum came from. It's called the *chicosapote* and is the sweetest fruit in the world. It does turn to sugar when it gets too ripe and you have to eat it before that happens. The people that live in the *Cenote* caves sell it for exorbitant amounts." He scooped up a spoonful from the thin tan skin and fed it to her.

"Jôn said it's almost unknown because it turns to sugar so quickly. He's really trying to spoil you. I should be jealous but now that you belong to the world, I can't be."

They savored the unknown tastes and finished off the hot chocolate. He slipped in beside her on the C.H.A.R. and they both dozed off again.

L'ora woke first and reached up to circle his neck. "Take me to bed, Scotty."

He looked at her, "Don't use up your strength."

L'ora pulled off the empty Limpet bag stuck to her neck. A small red circle remained beside the other two adjoining it. "After three bags of nutrients, a feast and two cups of delicious chocolate milk, I think I have enough strength for a good while." She pulled him down and kissed him, "I need your strength, love me, please."

He carried her to her cubicle and laid her on the new mattress, slipping in beside her to begin to unfasten her beautiful outfit.

"No, now!" she demanded and they began to respond to their innermost needs.

Much later, Scotty left her sleeping and slipped out to bring her the next courses that Jôn had programmed to send through the "Storage" room's food portals.

A smothering cover woke L'ora and she felt hands wrapping it around her body. Heart racing, she looked into the shaded eyeholes of the invader leaning over her as he pulled her wrapped body from the bed cubicle. A glance showed many white figures with high pointed hoods filling the small room. "Scotty! Scotty! Help!" she screamed as she wrestled within the confiding fur.

She saw her mate burst through the frame and throw himself on the white-robed men. The tall white-peaked throng that was resisting his desperate fight to get to her blocked her last sight of him as he fell to the floor.

"Don't take her . . . Leee!" she heard his anguished cry as she was rushed through the back frame onto the outside walkway.

"Consequentors!" she screamed as a flowery scent pulled her into a dreamless sleep.

Chapter 19

Consequentors

Dazed, L'ora felt the enormous thrust of pressure that pushed her body against the soft material on which she lay. *What happened? Where am I?* Then memory rushed in and despair gripped her mind, *Scotty! The Consequentors!* The pressure streamed her tears into the soft pillow under her head. She gasped and tried to breathe, her skin pulled back toward her ears and her lips opened against her teeth. The pressure suddenly disappeared and she floated up against a strong web that trapped her body and her tears floated up in front of her eyes. *I'm in space! That's impossible! No one goes to space! I've gone mad; everything has been a dream, a nightmare!* She watched her tears float together into tiny crystal balls that spun innocently in circles until suddenly she dropped back against the pad below her and her tears splashed softly against her cheeks. *Our child* was the next desperate thought and she pressed her hand against her skin, almost feeling the tiny threads of her silver tree. Somehow she knew, *it's all right, we're all right.* A cry burst from her into the dark, "Scotty!" and sobs again racked her body.

"Sir, she is awake." The neatly uniformed medic addressed his Senor.

The older man spun around in the power chair, "Is she well? Was there any chance that the sleeping drug or her struggles could have hurt her womb?"

"No sir, I gave her the lightest possible dose; in fact she was waking up even before we went into orbit. However, I think you need to reassure her as she is sobbing as if her heart was breaking." The medic smiled and touched the rapidly swelling purple bruise on his cheek. "Even malnourished, she is astonishingly strong. A very capable young woman and I wonder if that Silversuiter might be her mate. I never saw a man fight so hard. We have four of ours in the sickbay and all of us bear tokens of his strength."

"Did you leave him alive?"

"As you wished, we left him there; the palace army was approaching fast. I took a moment to check him and outside of a blow to his head, probably some smashed ribs and a broken arm, I think he will be all right. He fought so hard we had to fight back much harder than we had planned. Maybe we can "capture" him later and send him with the 'dead' ones we rescue."

"No, leave him there, as special guard to the Supreme, we need him to be within the central council to learn what they are planning. If they find him beaten and unconscious they will know how hard he tried to keep the Consequentors from taking the Mistress."

The Senor strode toward the command quarters, his neat midnight blue uniform showing no sign of his authority outside of the thin silver circle around his cuff. He covered them with the medic's white costume robes and carried the long pointed hood in his hand.

The frame opened and he slipped in, dropping the white material on the nearby skeleton of a chair. For a minute he gazed at the fur-wrapped figure in the bed cubicle, still held down by the launch net. He retracted the web and the net lifted off her body. Touching her trembling shoulder he whispered, "Don't worry Mistress Lee, you are safe now."

Karlos and Joana rushed into the cubicle, answering Scott's emergency signal. "Scott," Karlos cried, dashing to the limp body. Relieved, he saw his friend's hand twitch.

Joana grabbed his arm, "Boots down the hall!" she warned and pulled him out of the frame. They managed to duck into the "Storage" frame just in time.

"They're using the foot solders, not the Silversuiters." He whispered in her ear, "And L'ora is not there! I must check back to my post and find out what is happening. Go to the main console and I will beam you every ten minutes. Keep contact with Jôn at all times and let him know if I miss a beam." A loving hug and he was gone out through the back toward the hidden pods and she ran to the master controls.

A part of the wallcast displayed a team of medics rushing into L'ora's cubicle and the hidden interior eye Scott had recently placed showed them strapping his limp body onto a floating stretcher. A tall thin medic gestured for them to take him out toward a large medical pod floating beside the emergency rail. He turned to go and his entire face filled the wallcast. Joana gasped at the cruel look of pleasure the medic gave when looking at the wounded Silversuiter being flown out of the cubicle.

Jôn's voice broke in, "That's Mancera, I'll do what I can to make sure he has to give Scott up to the Council as soon as they get to the Golden Palace. We don't want any of ours in *his* hands."

Chapter 20

Operation Wrist Control

The sharp pain woke Scott into full consciousness and he tried to sit up against the straps that held him down. He jerked his arm, causing a stabbing pain to add to several others in his body. "What are you doing?" Scott shouted to the medic holding his wrist while trying to grab a scalpel that was buried deep in the silver flesh above his control panel. He strained to get two fingers on the medic's wrist and that was enough. "Unfasten me, NOW!"

The medic tried to let go of Scott's wrist but the Silversuiter's commands brought his nerves under control before he could pull away. "You weren't supposed to wake up for another hour!" he shrieked, "I would have had it by then." He mentally resisted but had to follow the commands that now locked his nerves to Scott's and he unfastened the straps that held the Silversuiter's body to the medical floater.

Scott looked at the bloody gashes around his arm and at the scalpel still grotesquely sticking from his forearm. "You were trying to cut my control from my arm!"

He sat up and looked at the medic. "Answer me, what is your name and explain what you were doing."

The thin medic tried not to answer but the silver commands controlled his body and he stammered, "I, I wanted your control for myself. You Silversuiters are already too powerful and I want to control everyone as you do. I am Chief Medic Mancera and am the exclusive attendant in charge of the Supreme Teacher's team. Sometimes he needs me to do things that the Silversuiters will not do because of their ridiculous oaths."

Scott's anger rose at some of the thoughts Mancera opened to his vision of the X rack and its victims. "Take me to the Supreme, I am his personal guard." Feeling the fear in his captive, he continued, "I will tell Supreme of your attempt to become stronger than he and we'll see what he thinks of that." He stood up, keeping his fingers around Mancera's wrist as he discovered his useless left arm and the pain in his side as he breathed. Looking into Mancera's cruel eyes, he realized that the slightest loss of control over the medic would bring instant consequences. "March!" he commanded and followed the medic out of the door with the medical emblem etched into the glass.

They walked down numerous corridors and Scott gasped as he began to feel his strength waning. He tightened his grip on his captive and realized that the medic was trying to wear him down. "Take me by the most direct route, not all over the palace."

The medic's smile disappeared and he answered. "Of course, we are now far from the Council room. You won't make it; my cut in your arm is bleeding your strength away. I will be able to finish my work on your control before we get there." His face showed his anger at having to reveal his plan to overpower Scott and take his master control.

Scott tried to use his other hand to open his controls but the broken bones remained limp and he dared not let Mancera loose. He deliberated trying to pull the scalpel out with his teeth but feared the blood would flow even faster. He thought of L'ora, captive of the Consequentors, and the anger and fear for her brought renewed strength to his body. "March!" he directed again, and used his body to push the medic in front of him. His mental control forced Mancera to revel the shortest paths to the council chamber. As he felt his strength draining, he commanded, "Push the small orange button on my control."

Helpless to disobey, Mancera did has he was ordered and immediately a voice rang out, "Commander Fourth, where are you?"

"Answer," Scott ordered. His mental control forced Mancera to revel where they were.

They heard the rapid footsteps of Silversuiters approaching but Scott's waning strength could no longer keep his body upright. He sank to his knees and then to the floor. Mancera pulled away from his grasp and ran down the nearest corridor. His comrades rushed up and he managed to say, "Catch the medic . . . Take me to the Council Room," before he blacked out.

A buzz of anxious voices woke him and he looked into the face of the Supreme. The lack of pain and the glimpse of medics on his side indicated that he was being cared for right in the Council Room.

"Where have you been and what has happened?" The Supreme said in a shrieking voice. "Where is the Mistress?"

Scott looked up, distress and pain written on his face. The words were almost too difficult to say. "I don't know... I was able to track her to her residential complex and finally to her cubicle just when Consequentors broke in and they must have taken her. I fought as hard as I could but they were just too many." He closed his eyes and the terrible memory racked his being as he tried to get up. "We must try to find her before they do something terrible to her."

A medic held him. "Wait until the plastibond sets. You've got blows all over your body; several broken bones and you need to rest until the meds take effect. You have lost a great deal of blood and we are only just beginning to replenish it." He tried to hold Scott down but, even weakened, the Silversuiter was too strong.

Scott looked at the Supreme. "A general alarm must go out NOW! The responses must be gathered of anyone noticing anything strange. It's not necessary to say how she was taken, only that the Consequentors have her."

A young Silversuiter looked at Supreme who nodded in agreement, "She must be found. Sound the alarms on all wallcasts." Supreme looked at Scott with an anxious expression. "Why did you tell your comrades to catch Mancera? What did he do?"

Scott looked at his arm where clear plastipatch sealed the deep incision just over his wrist control. "He was trying to cut my control off so he could use it to become the Supreme ruler."

Shocked, the Supreme stepped back. "He must be found also, and taken care of." He looked at the other council members, "He has secrets of our council. That is treason and the penalty is instant death."

The council members looked at each other and nodded, each murmuring shocked comments of personal acts that were their deepest and darkest secrets.

"He treated our victims after we were finished with them", one of the few younger men said as his sinister expression told how he had enjoyed the treatments he had given their captives.

"He knew everything we did and was a good enough medic to keep them alive long enough for the Consequentors to wring out whatever more they could say," another said, "He even knows about what happened when we tried that last sweep of the women's younglings from the Southern farms. He treated our survivors."

"We've been too greedy," an older man reflected, "The Teacher's Lounge used to be full of women and he knows what happened to the ones that didn't escape into freezing death with their children."

"Mancera knows too much about all of us. He must be eradicated."

Chapter 21

A Trip to the Unknown

L'ora looked at the face of the older man in the neat uniform. "Where am I? . . . Am I truly in space? . . . Where are the Consequentors? Did you catch them?"

He looked at her and she felt his compassion in the soft touch of his hand on her arm and the expression of reassurance in his eyes. "Do not fear, my lovely Lady, we are going to the safest place on the planet, where all will care for you."

L'ora looked into his eyes and suddenly trusted him. "Fourth, my partner, is he alive and with you? He attacked the Consequentors but there was too many of them. Please, tell me he is alive." She sat up in the bunk and looked around, seeing the material covering the chair. Shocked, she pulled back against the cold metal wall of the bunk as she had done

—could it have been such a short time ago?—,

when she had lived another life. "You are a Consequentor! You tricked me!"

He smiled. "Don't worry Mistress Lee, the best disguise is to be dressed as someone feared by all. We have saved hundreds of those trapped by the Teachers and many of the captured women that tried to escape into the snow. They even turn over the ones that won't talk for us to wring secrets from them. We always say they died under questioning and tell whatever we want the Teachers to know about what the victims might have said. Many of them are alive and well."

L'ora could hardly believe his words. "But those strange costumes, why do you wear them?"

He smiled again, "In ancient States' history there was a time after a terrible war when some of the vanquished wanted to defend their families from the cruelties of some of the conquerors. They disguised themselves in robes and high peaked head coverings and attacked the unlawful elements of the new rulers."

L'ora couldn't help asking. "But why did you use their costume designs if they were in the right?"

"Because whenever a group hides their identity and acts against the law, they become lawless. Cruel and vicious members use their anonymous disguise to become worse than those they originally were trying to stop. The group becomes feared and with reason. People don't dare stand up to those that wear that disguise, especially if the rumor is spread that they are extremely brutal and murderous. That has been our cloak of invisibility right in the middle of these most dangerous dictators. None of our people are allowed to wear the robes more than a few times and then usually to a rescue where they know the territory."

"But Scotty, I saw you beating him, why?"

"That wasn't planned, we had no idea you would be instantly protected by such a warrior. Our contact had him distracted in the 'Storage' room and we never dreamed that he would get to you so soon. How did you warn him?"

"The Silversuiters "hear" me when I call out in danger . . . But you are telling me that Jôn is your contact, not that of the Supreme? And he set up the trap for you to capture me? But why did he betray us? We trusted him."

"We wanted the Teachers to think that the Consequentors had taken you. They fear us and will gather all of their strength to try and fight us to get you back, which is what we want. We think we are now strong enough to defeat their army. Since they haven't found our base, we will be able to pick the terrain."

"But Scotty?"

"Our medic assured me that he is hurt but will get well quickly. The Silversuiters are the strongest and healthiest humans on the planet."

"Please let him know I'm all right."

"As soon as the Supreme accepts that Scott followed you to bring you back and that he tried to protect you. He will be questioned and it must be clear that he thinks that the terrible Consequentors have you and that he doesn't know where you are. Rest now as we are coming out of sub-orbit." He gave her a sip of some warmed sweet drink and fastened her net down again, "You'll need this."

L'ora sunk back into the soft pad and drew the warm furs around her. *Their enemies her friends? . . . And her friend allied with those she thought her enemies?* She felt her world turned upside down again *. . . "Scotty,"* she murmured as she found herself slipping into a restless slumber.

The sensation of floating awoke L'ora as her body pressed against the soft web that held her in the sleeping cubicle. She looked up quickly as the door opened on her answer to the knock of the young man that floated in to her side.

"Mistress Lee, our plans have changed as a sudden storm has prevented our shuttle from landing you close to Blue Ice City. You will have to go by boat from where we can land. Please come with me." He respectfully bent down, unhooked her net, and offered a steadying arm as she floated out of the cubicle. "Come quickly as the storm is only a few klicks away from your route."

L'ora was rapidly fitted with a pressure suit and loaded into a small shuttle pod which took off immediately from the larger vessel and headed toward the blue horizon and the white clouds below it.

Fascinated, she watched every minute of the descent of the shuttle pod until it scorched its way through the atmosphere and started their descent toward the white land ahead.

They landed down a lengthy white runway and a pod met them at the end. A heavy fur coat replaced the pressure suit and the fur on the hood almost covered her face. Thick boots with the fur inside were slipped over the thin kid foot coverings of the bodysuit she had worn for the presentation.

"Hurry Mistress Lee, the storm is upon us," a fur-covered young man said as he helped her cross the short distance to the open pod.

The blowing wind was even stronger than the blizzard on her birthday. By the time the door slid shut, she could feel the ice on her lips and see icicles around the heavy fur hood.

The pod shot off, throwing her back on the cushioned seat beside the young pilot who was fighting to keep his airpod under control. They flew up through the heavy blanket of clouds and she saw the controls that showed they were headed north. Soon the clouds became thinner and finally a weak sun shown on the ice-covered plateau above the coastline below. The young man who had helped her spoke to the pilot, "That was some takeoff Okhi, I'll never be that good."

"Aleksandr, you are just as good. We've got to get far enough ahead of the storm for Mistress Lee to get to Blue Ice by boat. We can't take a chance on someone tracking us."

"By boat? Great Gaia, that's too dangerous! Besides, I get seasick."

"You'd better not, she needs protection, and you're it."

L'ora finally got a chance to ask some questions. "What is Blue Ice and why isn't it on any of our master controls?

"No one's told you where you're going?" Aleksandr said in surprise. "Blue Ice City is the largest community on the planet. It's huge; a natural lava tunnel that goes deep into volcanic caverns in the earth. You'll be safe there although it looks like our training is finally going to be used. We don't think those "Teachers" are going to give you up without a fight."

Before she could ask any more, the pod shot down toward lights that appeared and lighted a long white strip in the snow. As the sleds touched down, L'ora realized that it was a regular landing field under a camouflaged white cover. Again there was a small group waiting for the pod. This time they rushed her to a group of three sleds, all pulled by dog teams. She and Aleksandr were quickly tucked into the sleds and the whining of the dogs signaled that they were straining to go. A call and they were off, racing toward the edge of the plateau. Before they had gotten far, they watched the pod lift off and shoot away from where they had unloaded.

L'ora saw the dogs heading the sleigh toward what looked like the edge of a sheer cliff. They barked as they raced toward the bluff and she caught her breath as she saw the lead dogs drop out of sight. Her sleigh tilted over a ledge and then slid onto a long wide ramp twisting out of sight under the side of the cliff. The tall fur-covered figure standing behind her leaned on a long brake pole to keep the sled from sliding into the racing dogs as they ran under the carved-out ledge that kept them invisible from any electronic eye that might be peering from above.

The weak light shown blue as she tried to see through the thick icicles that covered the outside of the ledge, making it seem as a long tunnel that sloped down along the cliff edge. Finally she saw the arched end of the passageway open onto a small cliff-surrounded cove where a boat was moored to a tiny dock. The dogs seemed to know exactly how close to get to the edge of the dock before they stopped and instantly curled up on the snow-covered wood.

Aleksandr ran up but her tall fur-covered driver had already lifted her out of the sled and before she could stand, she found herself flying through the air into the strong hands of another figure on the boat deck.

Aleksandr and her tall sled driver ran across the dock and jumped on the deck of the vibrating boat. A few wrapped packages were thrown across and the boat shuddered into motion and cut through the waves toward the mouth of the narrow cove. As soon as they emerged into the dark sea they were tossed by fierce waves that their sturdy boat climbed and mastered.

L'ora turned to the robust figure that was strapping a thick vest on her. "What kind of craft is this that can't lift off and makes such a loud throbbing sound? And who are you?"

"I'm Logi. I'm from Blue Ice City. The ancients made this boat and their machinery makes no impression on the electronic searchers. The brave men of this icy land have kept them working all these years. When it became essential to not leave any electronic trace we found them most useful to go back and forth to Blue City without being traced. You being on it with the storm upon us is dangerous but we cannot use the pods when the waves are high. This ship can go in and unload just outside the first frame. City's weather frames must be at maximum strength to deflect some of the wind."

He managed to grab her as a huge wave washed over the deck. "The storm is close, we must hurry." He unwound a long henequen rope and tied it around her waist and onto a large ring bolted on the side of the cabin. "The knot can be untied quickly by pulling on this end of the rope." Slipping the holster of a knife into her boot, he said, "This is a woman's knife, it is *kinaktok*, very sharp. If for some reason we start to sink and you cannot untie this knot, you must cut the rope. I'll be right beside you but you must be prepared. We can't go inside the engine cabin, it would be a coffin if the boat is rolled over."

The next giant wave hit her in the back and pitched her off her feet into the arms of giant Logi. He held her tight while holding onto the iron ring and her arm grabbed into his fur collar, touching his neck.

"You're a Silversuiter!"

"No, not me, I'm a Silverson. How did you know that?"

"I don't know what a Silverson is but I can 'feel' Silversuiters and sometimes they can 'hear' me. What's a Silverson?"

He smiled, his voice echoing his pride "My father was a Silversuiter and all of us have some of the powers of the Silversuiters. Some of the skin over our veins looks silver."

"All of you? How many are there?"

"Well, there are more of us younglings here in Blue City than all the Silversuiters that we know of. All the children from the farm compounds are fostered here before they are twelve and many of them had Silversuit fathers."

"Are there any Silverdaughters? Do they have special powers also?"

"We don't know. More of the children of the Silversuiters are boys but the ones that are girls don't show any silver on their skin. They are equally healthy and grow tall." He blushed, "And they are very beautiful."

L'ora teased him, surprised at her unaccustomed audacity, "You have a special one."

Logi blushed again, "Yes, Vala's father was a Silversuiter. We will be the first pair of Silverchildren to Bond. It will be a very special ceremony. We are hoping it will be soon."

Logi deposited her on a small bench fixed below the ring and ran to the side rails of the ship where Aleksandr was clinging to a rope that came from a pulley on the stark mast. He grabbed their companion just before the next wave washed him overboard. Carrying him back to where L'ora sat, he commented, "He's seasick, I'll keep him here, he can't hold on against the waves." He looked at the figure in his arms, "Alek, are you better?" He smiled at L'ora, "There's no water near his homeland, only ice."

Logi swept a handful of clean snow from the flat roof of the tiny engine room and gave it to Alek. "Put this in your mouth and let it melt. An icy stomach will help you. A hotshot pilot like you can't be doubled over when the trouble starts and it will be any day now. What's your gunner Rashida Naghibzadeh going to say? She'll never stop teasing you." He looked at L'ora, "War's coming and you're the catalyst."

L'ora looked back, "Nobody understands, I'm just an archivist. Without my partner's strength, I can't be in a battle, or lead people."

He looked at her, "You're the one that doesn't understand. You already are our leader and you must not fail us."

She shrunk down on the small bench and drew her furs around her. *The entire world is falling on my shoulders, Scotty, where are you? I need you so. Send me your strength.*

The boat chugged on toward the huge icy blue glacier cliffs. The advantage of a swift current helped speed them on their way.

Chapter 22

The Consequentors' Caverns

Logi seemed not to notice L'ora's silence and chatted on about his home. "You'll really like Blue Ice City, it was one of the first populated after the Maelstrom. During the years it's grown and grown and is now almost as big as some of the ancient cities. Being so far underground and because of the natural minerals in the volcanic stone, the Supreme's forces haven't been able to find it. I'm from one of the Iceworm provinces; they are the oldest parts of Blue City. The Saviour and your ancestor sent the inventor of the force screens there to develop the force frames that everyone uses. The ones we have are the most advanced; and, used in tandem, can keep out a lot of the cold. When storms like this one hit, we have to use all of them and the city still gets icy blasts. That's when we can't let the pods fly in. We wouldn't have risked bringing you in by boat if you didn't have to be presented when the Council convenes tomorrow. The Senior leaders are presenting their war maps and need to show where they want you placed. The operation's command code name is Arch and your title is 'Joan of the Arch'. It has something to do with ancient history and a woman battle leader. My leading squadron is coded 'Joan's'."

Logi didn't notice L'ora's shocked look through the furs that surrounded her face. *Great Gaia, give me Scotty's strength and don't let me fail. How can I face real leaders without him? They'll know I'm afraid, — Scotty, help me.*

Logi's arm reached down and helped her up. "We're coming into the Iceworm now. Watch how cleverly the ancients used the magma tunnel beside the glacier."

L'ora looked around, "The waves are calmer and I didn't even know it."

"Well, that certainly shows you're not sea bred," he said, teasing her. "We outran the storm's front a while ago. It's just as well, we don't want big waves when we go under the shelf and I'm going to need Alek when we step down the mast."

"Step down? How?"

He grinned at her again, "People that haven't lived with the sea the ancients called 'landlubbers'. Today, we call the ones who have never traveled on the sea or in orbit-ships 'lubbers'. So you are a lubber."

Unexpectedly, Logi blushed and, embarrassed, stepped back. "Pardon me, My Lady. I forgot who you are. I am so ashamed of myself. Please forgive me . . . I'm mortified. Is it too much to ask that you not tell anyone?" He turned and called to Alek as he backed away from her, "Come Alek, I need you to help with the wheel."

L'ora watched Logi run away, pulling Alek beside him. The two headed to the stern of the boat where the third man was holding onto a large wheel with many spiked handholds around it. She could see that the heavily furred man had been steering the boat and she watched as he pointed toward a large ice cliff and left Alek the steering wheel.

Logi and the shorter man pulled large wooden wedges out of a thick metal collar around the mast, freeing it to slip down around its base. The shorter man grabbed the ends of three rigging ropes attached to the top of the tall mast. Logi managed to steady two of them while the other man loosened the third. The mast slowly tipped over, dropping down onto fixed curved blocks on one side of the deck. As soon as the mast was safely resting on the wooden supports, they closed curved blocks over them, locking the mast securely in place.

The unknown man made a comment that L'ora understood. She replied in his language, "That was very difficult."

The two men turned and stared at her. "What did you say?" Logi said as if she had spoken a language from another world.

L'ora repeated her statement and added in the Inuktitut language. "Why are you so surprised? My father helped me learn several languages and he said this one was going to be the most important. My name is Lee, what's yours?"

"Akiak, . . . It means *brave*," the fur-covered person said, his face revealing his Inuit-Inupiaq heritage.

She nodded, having understood what his name meant.

Alek came up behind them. "Does anyone know you speak that language?"

"No, why?"

"Keep it a secret and only tell it at the council, it is a great gift for our cause. But come, Logi is spreading out the canvas."

He motioned with his hand and, before helping her lie flat on the folded canvas at the bow of the vessel, he pointed toward the huge glacier coming up swiftly in front of them. "See the dark spot on that side? We're going in there. Keep your head down, we can't afford to lose you."

The boat churned toward the glacier face and suddenly the light turned blue. L'ora's teeth started chattering and the icy walls surrounding her made her feel colder than ever before. She saw Akiak's mitten holding onto the edge of the boat and realized he was outside of the bow on a small platform at the water level. The boat shuddered and then began speeding in a straight line down the icy tunnel on the glacier's side.

"We're joined to the mooring pulley," Alek said, "from now on it's swift. We're being pulled to the inner dock. You can look up now; the ceiling is higher here.

The pods can only get in this way when the sea is calm."

L'ora sat up on her knees and watched the sides of the tunnel speed by. In a few minutes they arrived at the mouth of a black tunnel where Akiak stepped off and moored the boat to a small wooden dock.

"This is a lava tunnel and our ancestors of over a hundred years ago enlarged and joined many of them," Alek said. They called their tunnels "iceworms", and lived in a place called Camp Century.

The ancients made kilometers of tunnels but the glacier was moving faster than they planned and some of the man-made tunnels were being squeezed so they abandoned the place."

"When the Maelstrom hit the world, and hordes of survivors tried to flee to the icy lands, Akiak's people got word to the Mistress's family and they brought hundreds of refuges that had families and some that had worked in the silver threads cavern. Akiak can tell you tales of how Ice Blue City was started when the people that lived in Camp Century discovered the natural caverns under the old volcanoes."

He swept his hand in courtesy, "Come with me, we have to walk through the weather frames."

L'ora walked down the gangplank and toward the way he indicated. They passed through three round thick frames and after each one the air got warmer. By the time they passed the last one they were carrying bundles of unneeded furs and the air was cool and no longer freezing.

Why do they treat me like some kind of ancient royalty? Logi won't even look at me; he's so mortified that he talked to me as a friend. I liked him as a friend, and now he won't even walk near me. At least Alek doesn't act like that.

They got into strange looking open pods that rested on tracks and soon were speeding down the tunnel. Her old fear of her building pods came back and she shut her eyes tightly and concentrated on not letting them see her fear. The pod slowed down and she opened her eyes and looked around in amazement.

"Alek, it's huge! I can't see the end of the city and there are caverns and tunnels going in all directions. It's beautiful but why is everything blue?"

"I told you you'd be surprised. During Spring and Summer, much of the light is filtered through the glacier to keep the city hidden. Wait till you see the military caverns where we're training. You'll see some of them tomorrow when you go to the Council meeting."

"Why doesn't the city get squeezed like the ancient's tunnels did?"

"These are built in rock inside the old volcanoes and many were built to mine the rich ores that are in these mountains. The tops of the caverns have metals that deflect any spy beams sent to find settlements not under the Supremes' power. The lava tunnels are all surrounded with solid lava rock and hardened metals. The light tunnels dug into the glaciers have flexible fiber optic cables that are just below the surface of the ice and convey blue light throughout the cities."

"How many caverns are there?"

"A lot, I don't remember how many. You'll have to access an arm control to find out."

L'ora drew in her breath; *this is so big, how can I be in the center of it all? Scotty, Scotty, are you all right?*

She turned to Logi, looking him in the eyes, and said, "Your city is beautiful. Later you must show me around and let me meet your Vala. Please be my friends, I feel so lonely here and my partner is wounded and so far away. We were to be Bonded this week." Unexpected tears came to her eyes, "I don't know when I'll see him again. Imagine if Vala was lost from you."

Logi's cold expression changed, "I'm sorry, My Lady, I didn't realize how you must feel having been snatched from your friends and partner. I will call Vala to come and be company for you."

Chapter 23

The Supreme's Plans

Scott awoke in a dark room, the pain in his bruised body telling him that the medications had worn off. *How long has Lee been in the hands of the Consequentors? What are they doing to her?* The pain in his heart was worse than all the blows he had received. *Lee, L'ora, my love,* his anguish moaned.

A tiny, far away voice fleeted though his mind, *--Scotty, help me–* and then it was gone. He sat up, *that was her, I feel it. She's alive*! The thought brought both relief and fear. He put his head in his hands and concentrated, *Lee, Lee, where are you?* For a fraction of a second his mind looked out on vast white-crested waves washing against a huge jagged glacier, then light flooded the room and it was gone.

A medic hustled in, pain patches in her hand. "Commander Fourth, you must rest, lie down and go back to sleep." She reached out to gently push him back on the bed while her other hand swiftly pasted a patch by his plasticast. The effect was immediate, he resisted, but sleep flooded his body and he slipped back into darkness.

Scott's time sense awakened him several hours later and he stretched to throw off the effects of the sleeping drug. He felt his mental control returning throughout his battered body. The predawn grey of the sky outside his window slowly turned pink as the thick window-season projection portrayed the hues of an early spring dawn in a far-away latitude now only occupied by the older women farmers.

The night medic glanced in the door. "Commander Fourth, you mustn't be awake. You should sleep several hours more." She reached into the pocket of her uniform and brought out another patch. "The doctor sent word on the wall cast that you were to have your patch every three hours."

Scott sat upright and slipped out of bed, grabbing his tunic from the nearby peg. "What doctor? What medication is that?" He took her by the wrist and she answered as he had feared.

"His face did not appear on the 'cast but it was from the highest level," she replied under his control. "Your pain meds are special triple strength. The medic said that the Silversuiters needed much larger doses."

"You will not obey any medics' orders concerning my case. You must give me no more medication, do you understand?"

The medic nodded, and released, ran from the room.

Scott finished dressing and left the medical compound, painfully crossing the central plaza and into the main entrance of the Brain Palace. His wrist control enabled him to pass through the multiple heavily guarded checkpoints and enter the Supreme's Council room. Walking through the bunched councilors he stood at parade rest behind The Supreme. *I'm the only Silversuiter in the room*, he thought.

He watched the assembly members thronged around the council table, concentrating on the large CG-glass in the middle of the huge conference table. *Are they planning to rescue Lee? Have they learned something I don't know?*

Then the faint cry resounded in his head again.

—Scotty, come help me! —

He took a deep breath and concentrated on her very being. *—Lee, where are you? —*

A fleeting glimpse of a magnificent blue city in a huge cavern raced through his mind. The voice of the Supreme broke through his amazing vision.

"Commander Fourth, our trackers have picked up trails centering on this remote part of the Arctic. We think this might be the traitorous Consequentor's hideout and General Cirk'an thinks we should attack immediately before those treacherous disloyal murderers increase their number. The group of Consequentors you saw was the largest anyone has ever seen so our forces outnumber them and should be able to overpower them."

Scott looked down on the council table wallcast. He drew in his breath as he again saw the ice-bound cliff that walled the edge of the enormous glacier. "I agree with the General, we must prepare to strike." —*Lee, love, am I sentencing you to death or to rescue?*

The Supreme seemed to draw strength from preparations for battle. "General Cirk'an, prepare your battle forces and report to me as soon as ready. Commander Fourth, collect the still loyal Silversuiters and see how many we can count on. You command one group and Second the other. Third has turned traitor and we don't know where he is. Your Silversuiters will lead the attack."

That's one way to find out which of the Silversuiters are loyal, thought Scott ruefully.

Supreme continued his commands. He spoke to one of the council members, "Check with Jôn about that place, I think he comes from an ice camp near there."

Scott thought, *and he betrayed me so that Lee could be captured.* "Supreme Leader, let me contact him on the protected guardroom 'cast, we have worked before on orders for your events."

"Granted, now go."

"Sir, what about that deceiving medic? He ordered that I be kept drugged and must be still in the building. Silversuiters should be sent to question the medics and find out where he is hiding."

"Yes, and arrest any that followed his orders."

Scott tried to jog down the corridor toward the portal to the Teacher's Lounge but a long stride was the best he could manage. "Karlos," he said with relief, seeing his friend guarding the entrance. "What have you heard from the Constitutionalists?"

"They are gathering forces from every community in the world that still has serviceable long distance pods and Troms II in ancient Norway has kept them fueled. All are headed toward the glacier."

"How do they know about the glacier? The Supreme just found out and his army is only beginning their battle plans."

"There's much you need to know and you are in no shape for a battle. *You* are our secret weapon as you can keep us informed of the Supreme's plans while you recover."

"Karlos, I '*heard*' Lee, she is at the glacier. How can it be attacked without killing her?"

Karlos slipped an arm under his shoulder and helped him up the stairs to the guard center. "I don't think you have to worry so much, Joana tells me that she has been shown that the installations there were built far underground and are well protected. We need to keep in constant contact so that you can transmit the Supreme's battle plans to our forces. We have a contact inside the cavern city and he can contact us at all times. He says that Lee is fine and will be speaking to the Central Council right now. The Council ordered the Consequentors to bring her to them."

Scott looked puzzled. "I don't really understand, how are those two groups in contact? Aren't they enemies?"

Karlos eased him into the guard's panel seat and turned him toward the huge wall cast. "Contact Jôn, he can tell you better and Joana has much news for you. The best thing is that Lee Is safe and with you being part of the battle plans; we can keep her that way. Third has already left with the Silversuiters he was able to contact."

"Jôn . . . that traitor . . . he betrayed Lee into the Consequentors' hands and tried to keep me from saving her."

"No, Scott, he was trying to keep you safe and have her taken to the safest place of all. Relax here and watch the guard wallcast. Connect with Joana and let her tell you what has happened. I'll get to Commander Second and keep you up on the attack plans."

Chapter 24

The War Council

L'ora slipped her arms into the silken robe that Vala held out for her. The tall girl smiled as she tied it with a thick braided cord, "All of my clothes are far too big for you. This is the smallest dress outfit I could find in such a short time."

L'ora looked in the oval mirror gracing the wall of the elegant room where she had spent the night. "It's beautiful but I have never seen a design like this."

"It's part of a Bonding dress used by a family from the Northern Japanese Islands. They were rescued but the groom succumbed to the bacteria before they could have the Bonding ceremony. The pilot that brought you was from that family. Okhi and Alek will be flying the pod squadrons beside my Logi's. She blushed, "Twenty-four hours was all we had before he left on maximum alert." Tears filled her eyes, "Gaia keep him safe, I feel our Bonding date is near."

"—Come, your pod is waiting. May Akna, the goddess of childbirth of the ice people, protect you."

L'ora squeezed her hand as they walked down the cavern steps. "Maybe we can have our Bonding together, Gaia willing."

They walked out the carved entrance of the building and L'ora realized that the entire complex was carved out of living stone. She waved good-bye and climbed into the large pod that immediately charged down the shining metallic tracks.

Beside her Akiak turned, motioning her to silence. Speaking in his language he whispered, "We must not let anyone else know that you speak my tongue. I have advised the council and some of our plans have changed. My brother is a Cadet Silversuiter and is now headed to the Palace to seek word of your Silversuiter. We are twins." He stopped as the pod rushed into a long Iceworm tunnel where all sounds were magnified back and forth.

L'ora blinked at the bright blue light as the pod emerged from the tunnel and then gasped as she looked down. "Akiak there's an army down there with squadrons of fighter pods! And there's Facil's Constitutionalists marching up the road toward us!"

The pod stopped in front of a wide staircase climbing to beautifully carved columns. Akiak took her elbow as they reached the large balcony overlooking the military preparations.

"We only have a short time before the teacher's forces attack. That wide Ice curtain will be melted when the time comes for us to send out our forces. Come, the Council is in session." He guided her through the ornate portal and into a high domed room. "This way," he said and they entered a huge room. "It's copied from the ancient Senate chamber of our States ancestors." He guided her toward the front of the half-moon room and up beside a small group of men that were seated there. He introduced himself, "Honored Leaders, I am Akiak, *Brave one.*"

Two men stepped out from behind the central podium and Akiak introduced them. "This is my eldest brother, Speaker Ataninnuaq, *one who councils and knows things*, and Senior General Kuvageegai, *one who loves his homeland.*"

"Welcome, Mistress Lee, you are just in time to address the council." Speaker Ataninnuaq led her up behind the podium and spoke to the crowded room. "Ladies and Gentlemen, members of the World Council, may I introduce our honored guest, Mistress R'oak, the direct descendant of the Saviour and the Mistress themselves. If all goes as planned, she will be the catalyst that lures the Teacher's forces into our trap." He stepped aside, leaving L'ora looking out over a sea of faces from all over the still populated places on the planet.

For a minute, she felt overwhelmed by the roar of applause that greeted her and panic froze her lips, *what shall I say? Of what kind of trap am I to be the bait?* Scenes flowed through her mind; of Vala and Logi and her new friends that had risked getting her to the council and of Scotty and the silver tree that covered her womb. *They trust me to help the world.* A new confidence flowed though her and spoke through her lips, "Honored members of the Council, Ladies and Gentlemen, Greetings," she said, "I am at your service for any task you wish for me to make."

It was enough, the applause rang out again, and Senior General Kuvageegai, stepped up and took her by the hand, helping her down beside Akiak.

Returning to the podium, his voice magnified through the room. "Our plan goes into effect immediately. Century City will now become visible from the enemy's spy pods and will be the center of their attack. They will see Mistress R'oak and will be lured into recapturing her. Everyone knows what to do."

Within minutes the room was emptied, even stately diplomats rushing out the wide doors. L'ora turned to Akiak, "What am I supposed to do?"

He put his hand on her waist and hurried her toward an exit. 'I'll tell you as we go."

Chapter 25

Treason

"That's what happened," Joana finished telling Scott over the closed channel of the wall cast. "Now Jôn needs to talk to you."

"Find Akiak's twin brother, Iluak," Jôn told Scott who was still amazed by the story of the Consequentors' disguise that Joana had just related. "He will keep you in secret touch with L'ora."

In touch with Lee, rang through Scott's mind. "All cadets from the Inuit peoples report to me immediately in the Supreme Council Room," he spoke through his wrist control as he maneuvered down the stairs and into the passageway to the Council Room.

When Scott entered the Council Room, the buzz of excited voices pulled him to the table cast.

"That old Century Camp is the Consequentors' hideout."

"We've got them now."

"Send the spy pod down closer, there are people coming out."

Scott saw two fur clad figures come out into the deep snow. A second glance fixed on the first one, making his heart race. Despite the heavy furs, he knew it was L'ora.

"The smaller one is a prisoner, he's being pushed along."

"The other's a Consequentor, even his fur hood is pointed."

"The snow's too deep, they won't make it to that escape pod."

The first fur-covered figure stumbled into a deep drift and struggled to pull out. Looking up, L'ora's face was visible to all as she saw the spy pod. She pointed up and her captor looked where she was pointing and saw the enemy's direct surveillance.

The group chorused, "That's the Mistress!"

Akiak leaned over and pulled L'ora from the deep snow. "I'm sorry, My Lady," he said. "My brother Iluak coded me that the council has seen us as we planned. I'll try not to hurt you." He pulled her again toward the building they had just left. Following instructions, she made a show of struggling and he seemed to hit her, dropping her back into the snow where she lay still. He threw her limp body over his shoulder and carried her back into the building.

Scott felt rage washing over him and his hands became painful fists. The short silver figure that appeared beside him saluted and introduced himself, "I am Iluak, *person that does good things*, Akiak's twin brother." He spoke swiftly, his voice scarcely audible. "We 'hear' each other and I can communicate with him mentally to turn on his controls. He says that what you saw was just Akiak and Mistress Lee acting so that the Supreme would send his army into the trap the World Council has prepared with the Constitutionalists."

Scott felt his rage abate. "Iluak, you're sure what you're telling me about her?"

Iluak did not answer, his attention drawn to the silver figure dashing into the room.

All eyes turned to Karlos who made a swift salute and reported disaster. "Supreme, sir, Commander Second has taken off in attack airpods with his command of Silversuiters. They have disabled many of our pods! The control tower operators were unconscious and the first Security team to find them also collapsed. Our Silversuit team managed to clear the air from the tower and the first operator to awaken said that Medic Mancera was with Commander Second!"

Scott didn't wait to hear more. With Karlos' support and that of Iluak, they raced toward the door. Passing the council, he gave Supreme his last command, "Supreme, Sir, send all your forces after them, I'll take my faithful Silversuiter fighter airpod pilots and try to cut them off." He was talking to his control before they cleared the door.

The Supreme's quivering voice called out behind them, "Stop! Who's going to protect us?"

Iluak winked at his companions; "He's going to need a lot more than our protection when the World Council gets him on trial."

Karlos continued his report, "Commander Fourth, they disabled your command pod and you need the speediest airpod."

Scott consulted a map on his wrist control and then turned the group toward another disguised guard passage, "This way, hurry!" His wrist control opened the frame and they rushed in. "I only hope Commander Second didn't think of this."

"The traffic controller told us that Commander Second seemed groggy and was being guided around by Mancera. Maybe that's from the pod crash he had last week," Karlos said.

"Of course! It's the medication they were trying to use on me. He's drugged!"

They rushed through several frame portals, each opening onto a more luxurious area. Finally the last one opened onto a red-carpeted terminal where a sleek airpod rested.

"That's the Supremes' private airpod!" Karlos exclaimed, "An X-15 Megasonic, and the only one ever made!"

"I can navigate, we are going to my homeland," said Iluak.

Scott waved his control at the pod and the side door obligingly opened and a carpeted stairway unfolded to their feet. "Hurry," he said, "we've got to get out of here before the controllers get organized."

They dashed up the steps and into the ornate airpod. The three strapped into the aeronauts' seats in the front compartment of the pod. "It's always ready for an emergency escape so hold on," Scott said, seeing Karlos already toggling the correct switches. The large hanger doors slid open and within minutes they were plastered to their seats by the rocketing takeoff.

Iluak scrolled through countless maps on the wall cast, piecing together a long string of detailed course sheets. "The ancients' Century Camp is not even shown but I grew up on the bay shore beside the glacier that hides the entrance to Blue Ice City.

Century Camp is farther inland on the glacier itself and there are towers with ladders to climb down into the ruins. The Camp tunnels lead into the mountain and some of them run into the tunnels that lead to the caverns where Blue Ice City is. We may have a time advantage as they will have to search for a way to get into them. Here are your co-ordinates."

Iluak began talking into his wrist control and both Karlos and Scott looked at each other. Despite the years of Silversuit Cadet training, they could not understand a word he was saying. He smiled at the expression on their faces, "Don't worry, almost no one in the world knows what I am saying." A woman's voice came on and he turned the volume as high as it would go then turned it off.

Scott felt his entire body reaching toward the voice although he understood nothing. "Lee," he said, "are you all right?"

Iluak said, "You must not speak to her. No one should hear anything except my people's dialect, which cannot be translated. We use twenty-seven words to describe snow and each one has a code meaning although a spy translator can only translate them as 'snow.' She says she is fine and that my brother Akiak is taking care of her. They are coming down the ladder to the maze of Iceworm tunnels that go from Century City Camp to Blue Ice City and through them is the way we have to go. Our ship is too big to go in from the sea cave and we must catch Mancera before he gets in through the Century City tunnels."

Chapter 26

Battle

The sleek airpod skyrocketed through the sub-orbit route that Iluak had laid out. They discussed several plans, none of which seemed feasible.

Karlos kept constant communication with Joana and she relayed Jôn's reports as each new piece of information came in from the spy pods, now controlled by their master computer;

—"Commander Fourth, your Silversuit squadron is thirty minutes behind you and the spy pods place Commander Second's Silversuit fleet about fifteen minutes ahead of you. They are on absolute silence and have no information about their Commander's plans. They think they are going after the Consequentors to rescue the Mistress." —

—Your Silversuiters without pods are guarding the palace and have the Supreme and his Council locked into their Council room without communication. —

—The entire army loyal to the Supreme is on large troop air pods and will arrive at what is now being called "ground zero" about the same time as your squadron. —

—Neither the Silversuiters in the Ice City tunnels with Commander Third nor your Silversuiters in the fighter pods want to fire on their companions under Mancera for they are innocent of any wrongdoing of their drugged Commander Second. We've discovered Mancera did the gassing of the control tower. —

—Commander Third and his Silversuiters are deployed with the World Council's ground troops inside the caverns." —

The three Silversuiters in the pod cabin looked at each other, "Kill their innocent companions?"

"Suppose Mancera is not just after L'ora but plans to destroy the resistance whether it kills her or not?" Scott said.

As the ships began to convene on "ground zero", Joana sent an emergency message to Karlos.

—"Your Silversuiters interrogated the medical department and have searched his wall cast files. Mancera has a map of the original Century City Camp and it includes the entrances to the Iceworm tunnels! —

Each minute brought them closer to Ice City where the World Council Troops and Airpod Force waited to annihilate the Supremes' army and the leading Silversuit attack pods.

Joana sent an urgent message; —Commander Fourth, your ship is fast catching up and is only a few minutes behind Mancera and Commander Second. He is coming down to land on the hidden pod aerodrome of Century City Camp! It looks like one of the Silversuit airpods is breaking off to follow him. The entire armed forces of the Supreme Professor are airborne in squadrons of giant cargopods accompanied by attack fighter pods and pod bombers. None of your Silversuiters have followed the Supremes' orders; they are in the attack pods behind you. One of your patrols is guarding the Brain Palace Council Room and all of Commander Third's command is inside Blue Ice City, deployed with the World Council's forces.—

Scott alerted his team, "Mancera's after Lee, prepare to land. Iluak, communicate with Lee and Akiak, find out where they are and warn them! Call the World Council Leaders to guard the tunnel entrances to the cavern cities."

Iluak's singsong words were answered by four voices, one of them a woman. After several excited unintelligible comments, only her voice could be heard. She talked rapidly and then cut off. Iluak translated, "Speaker Ataninnuaq and Senior General Kuvageegai report that Facil's Constitutionalists are deploying into the Iceworm tunnels but their forces are thin as they have to spread out between the many unused rifts."

"Come on man, what was Lee saying?"

"She is trying to mentally contact the Silversuiters in Mancera's fleet to warn them of his treason and the drugging of Commander Second."

"If any one can do it, Lee will be the one. Tell her to have the ones she contacts to pull off West so they will not be shot down. Gaia help her to save those innocent Silversuiters!"

They had started their landing approach when Joana's final warning came through. —"Mancera and an armed group dressed like medics have run to the above-ground conduit closest to the glacier. We've found some maps that show where the ladders down are located. You can see the maps of the tunnels on your controls and we'll send them to Third's Constitutionalists in the tunnels. Be careful, the Silversuit ship will be landing about five minutes behind you. We don't know if any of the troops know you are in the Supremes' private ship!"—

They came down fast, Scott braking at the last minute beside the indicated metal duct vent that led to the underground ice tunnels. The airpod skidded and fishtailed until it finally nestled into the deep drifts.

Fiber optic laser wands and assortments of modern weapons were divided among them from the well-armed airpod. Belts with neutron pistols, explosive heat-seeking snowballs and laser mine drillers circled their waists as they raced through the deep snow toward the large tube that led down into the Century City complex.

Iluak and Karlos rushed ahead, climbed up on the entrance tube and forced the wedged door open. Holding onto the vertical ladder inside the tube, they began their silent climb down.

Scott faced the ladder with both wounded arms. He tried several painful experiments and finally wormed down, gripping the sides of the ladder with his feet, knees and shoulder, steadying himself with the plasticast encased arm. The painful force shattered the cast around the deep cuts and forced him to jump the last part of the ladder, landing hard on the smooth bottom of a wide man-made tunnel that ended where a large natural cavern split out into three different directions.

"We split up," Karlos whispered to him through their controls, "we left you the left one of the three caves. Good luck,"

Controlling the pain in his arms and side, Scott ran silently down the natural tunnel, weaving in and out among the stalactites and stalagmites, his path lighted with the smallest ray of his fiber light wand.

When he rounded the second sharp curve he 'heard' a repetitive message in his mind,—*All Silversuiters, this is Mistress L'ora, Do not attack the Century Camp, it is a trap for the Supreme's forces by the World Council's army. It's the final step toward freedom for the world. Your orders are coming from Medic Mancera who has drugged Commander Second.—*

Scott broke into her mindcast,—*Lee, where are you? I hear you clearly—.*

She immediately answered,—*Scotty, look for the blue light,*—and then went back to her concentrated broadcast.

He disengaged the wand but all went black, as black as his worse nightmares. *Am I in the wrong tunnel? This one snakes around in all directions and seems to be getting smaller. Could Karlos and Iluak hear her?*

After each curve, he covered the wand but the nightmare black would return. Finally a sharp turn and the nightmare showed a glimmering of blue in the distance. Reaching the next turn, the blue became brighter and, in the distance, a cavern opened up with a blue ceiling above it. His heart pounded, "L'ora" he whispered as he approached, mindful of not breaking again into her concentration. His mind filled with her message and he found himself melding into her mind and joining the broadcast up through the ice ceiling above them.

Other voices came in and Silversuiters Iluak, Karlos, and Third added their projections to hers. First one and then another voice responded and Joana announced that the Silversuiters' attack pods were turning west with their communication fibers open.

Scott ran into the large cavern, its ice dome letting the blue light color the entire area below it. Dark blue fissures covered the walls and round iceworms tunneled out in several places. He glanced at them, recording their positions before his entire being concentrated on the small figure sitting in the middle and looking up at the blue ice above her, Akiak standing behind her in a protective stance. With silent steps, he walked to her and slipped his love into his arms. They pressed their cheeks together and projected the saving message to the Silversuiters in the last airpods. "L'ora" he breathed and their skin touched, magnifying their love to each other.

Akiak, embarrassed, left his guard position behind her and walked toward the nearest Iceworm tunnel. A gasp and Scott and L'ora saw him fall, his attacker ducking back into the group of 'medics' pouring out of the tunnel. Seeing their prey, they pulled out their weapons.

"Kill him, not her!" Mancera shouted from behind them.

Scott pushed Lee toward a crevice in the limestone wall and fired his fiber weapon, not at the attackers, but at the blue ceiling above them. He dived to cover her as the attackers ran into the rain of glass-like ice spikes falling on them from the high dome above. A thick chunk of ice struck him on his shoulder and head and he collapsed half into the crevice.

L'ora kneeled over Scott's limp body and tugged at the large sheet of ice covering his back. "Scotty, Scotty," she cried, tears slipping down her cheeks.

A movement across the cavern caused her to look up. Shocked, she saw Mancera's long legs walking over the ice-stabbed bodies of his followers. He stood over her, "Well, my lovely, it´s just you and me. Not exactly how I planned it, but it will do nicely. Let's just make sure that your silver friend doesn't wake up and ruin it all."

He drew a knife and leaned toward Scott´s inert body. As he pointed it toward the vein pulsing in the silver neck, L'ora moved faster than she had ever done in her life. Pulling the woman´s *kinaktok* knife from its holster in her boot, she drove it up into the body of the unsuspecting medic and pushed him back onto a pile of the lethal ice shards. He gave her an amazed look, gurgled, and was still.

"Holy Gaia", Karlos said, running up, "are you the girl afraid to talk in public?" He knelt down beside Scott, touching his neck and feeling for a pulse. Scotty groaned and tried to turn over. "Don´t move Commander, you're OK and we´ll get you to a real medic right away." He gave L'ora another amazed look and spotted Iluak kneeling beside his brother. "Wait here," he said, standing up and running toward his companion, reporting into his control as he approached the twin brothers.

A dazed Commander Second stumbled into the open-roofed cavern, the stump of his control arm tightly bandaged. "There are the rebels," he said to the Silversuiters behind him, "get them."

L'ora stood up but before she could say anything, the Silversuiters were attacked from behind by Facil and the Constitutionalists. Their tall staves were swept sideways at the Silversuiters and the long strands of hair attached to the gilded knobs on the ends of the staffs wrapped around the silver bodies. Nets made of hair were thrown over the Silversuiters and hair ropes tied them securely.

Commander Second fell to his knees, and L'ora ran over to help him. "Don't worry Commander, these warriors have saved me, they are not your enemies."

He recognized her, "Mistress L'ora, is it all over?"

"Yes, Commander, all except getting everyone well."

A huge boom belied her words as they looked up through the hole in the glacier crust that had covered the dome. Above them, two great fleets of airpods broke formation and began to fight ship to ship. Huge bombs fell nearby and the cavern began to quiver with the vibrations. Pieces of the shattered dome began to crack and more icy knives began to rain around the sides of the cavern. "Quick, get everyone out of the cavern", Lee shouted, running to where Scotty was trying to stand. Ducking under his arm, she helped him to the Iceworm tunnel and returned to the dazed Commander Second who was stumbling after her. Putting her arm around his waist, she guided him around the ice knives that were falling from the slowly cracking remainder of the dome. Across the cavern, the Constitutionalists did the same with their bound Silversuit prisoners. Karlos and Iluak picked Akiak up and ran into the tunnel across from them. Small slivers of ice began to shoot everywhere so all went farther back into the safety of the curves of their tunnel.

"Just in time," Scott managed to say as a bomb dropped into the center of the cavern they had just vacated. Blades of ice glass shot into the tunnels and all pulled back into the fissures in the tunnel walls.

L'ora pushed into the large fissure that held Scotty upright. She hugged his body to her and their bodies joined in battle stance. "A great warrior you are, my Lady, and our son will be famous."

"You mean our daughter will be, don´t you?"

He put his hand over the silver tree that pulsed across her womb, "I think I mean both of them," he said. "Do we have to wait for the war to be over to have our Bonding?"

"I think we will have to share our Bonding ceremony, Vala was glowing yesterday."

Chapter 27

Airsquads

Arms entwined, Vala and Loki walked down through the violet-purple pre-dawn. The few streetlights, dimmed by the lack of solar energy in the early Spring northern realms, painted their faces a mournful shade that matched their innermost feelings.

"You're not crying, are you?" Loki asked, "You mustn't, everything will go just as planed."

Vala, her face buried in his uniform, quickly rubbed against his shoulder and looked at him. "No, of course not, we are ready." She paused, "I only wish we had another night."

He smiled, "We will have many such nights, something so wonderful can't just stop. He pushed her away a bit and looked at her. "You're gorgeous, you've always been beautiful but never so much as right now!"

She laughed, looking down at her rather-grimy jumpsuit. "Grease-monkey high fashion is the style of the moment among my friends." She paused, "I know what grease is, a sort of fish oil the Troms II complex sends us along with the fuel they smuggle us in the underwater pods. But what is a monkey?"

He laughed and hugged her then looked at the crowd at the trampod station. "Come on, or we won't get a seat." They pushed through the crowd, many couples still embracing or waving to those already boarded. They managed a last solitary seat and she sat on his lap, their tall bodies standing out among the packed transport. The normal buzz of voices was quiet; each knew the importance of the day's outcome. For some reason it had been named *D-day.*

As soon as they arrived, they shared a memorable kiss and each ran to their assigned places in the huge cavern dome, now packed with uniformed militia.

Logi joined Alek and Okhi and the other squadron leaders. Rashida Naghibzadeh was still kidding Alek about her pilot's seasickness. She looked at the group, "He went through pilot training, countless g's and can't stay up on a little boat. How can I expect him to fly me into battle?" They all laughed but instantly grew silent as Okhi gave them their latest orders.

Projecting the territory on their wrist 3-D screens, Okhi pointed out the entrance flight plan of their enemy and the latest estimates of their strength. "We have two main objectives: destroy the enemy, especially the troop ships, and make sure that no troop ships get into this cavern to deploy their troops. Since the Constitutionalists now have control of the cloud and the spy pods, we will have instant vision of their movements. Once the ice wall has been destroyed for our exit, this deployment area is Blue City's most vulnerable spot for an invasion. –Now, off to your pods and Gaia's luck to all!"

Logi climbed into his pod and began waving his hand over the pre-flight instruments as though he had not done so the afternoon before. Finally satisfied, he spoke to his gunner/navigator, "Pêro, is your check done?"

The shorter cadet waved a silver arm and gave a thumbs-up, ignoring the voice system. Then he said, "My brother Karlos is with Commander Fourth. They have a secret instant voice communication using Inuit language."

The green light flashing on his control board made him react and Logi began sliding their pod into position, they were to be the first off!

Once in the air, their first command was shocking, "Shoot down all the first Silversuiter Pods before they attack you. Do not shoot the Supremes' X-15 personal pod."

Pêro moaned, "Do they want me to shoot Karlos and our Silversuit comrades? Who's giving the orders and why?"

They flew on in silence, wondering the reason for the strange orders. Too soon, projections of the oncoming enemy pods flashed on their CG windows, the silver streaks of the Silversuit pods easily visible.

As they approached firing range, Pêro picked his targets, then, puzzled, he started shaking his head. "Logi, something's wrong. Do you hear a woman's voice? I hear something in my head, not on our communications."

"No, I don't hear anything," Logi started to say, then exclaimed, "That's Mistress Lee's voice! They listened to her directions and saw the oncoming Silver squadron's pods fall out of formation and begin to break up, some flying toward the western side of the glacier.

"I can hear my brother's voice!" Pêro said, "They are warning the Silver squadrons away!"

New directions came from their communications, "Leave the Silver squadrons alone and attack the Supremes' forces!"

The glass filled up with enemy pods, attack transports and those loaded with powerful bombs. Both Logi and Pêro gasped, they had not been able to imagine such numbers. The hornet's nest of the Council's pods behind them looked small compared with the enemy forces before them.

Before any visual sightings, Pêro begin firing, "We're almost out of range but firing first will disorient them, they're not expecting any real defense and think they will surprise us. They're flying so close together, they'll fly right into our barrage."

The multitude of explosions shown on their panels proved him right. All the Council's ships had followed his lead and the enemy attack force found itself flying into a wall of devastating destruction.

"Attack!" The command went out, "get them while they are disoriented."

"This isn't working" said Logi to his squadron leaders, as he again turned to fly in from the midday sun's weak beams. "The troop ships are getting through. Don't waist your energy going after the individual fighters, they don't seem to be well trained. We need to get the big guys. They seem to not know where Blue Ice City is, and are heading for Century City. We can't let them destroy our energy source." Those needing energy replacements fly back to Blue Ice in small groups, don't let any enemy ship follow you." He finished his run, seeing another huge ship plunge into the icy waters. "Good shot, Pêro, let's go back and fuel up, we've got just enough to get home and our projections aren't working any more."

As they approached their 'home' glacier and the huge cavern opening, they heard Okhi's shout, "Logi, behind and under you!" They weren't the target of the huge bomber flying in low behind them; it was heading straight for the open cavern where they had taken off that morning.

"Vala!" he thought as he turned his pod down toward the danger streaming toward his base.

Pêro shouted, "We have no energy left for our beams!"

Lugi pulsed the last energy in his pod and flew over the huge low flying attacking pod, then down until his pod was just in front above its control room. Their pod shook with the weak beams rained from the attacker but they also did not have the energy to finish them off.

"They're on visuals, their projections aren't working either," Pêro shouted, as they saw the pod beneath them waver in its trajectory.

Closer they flew, the bomber pod no longer in a straight line, its view covered by the two adjoining pods. They reached the Eastern side of their huge glacier and Okhi shouted, "Logi, get out of the way!"

Logi and Pêro watched incredulously as Okhi sat his pod down on top of the control glass at the front of the enemy pod, pushing its nose down toward the glacier just beneath them. They saw the huge pod waver, then dive directly toward the ice, carrying the small pod with it. The huge explosion shook them as they pulled up to avoid the racing flames pouring out of the deep crevice into which the huge airpod had flown.

The three returning lead squadrons used their last energy to fly across the glacier and into the huge cavern, their pilots shaken and mourning the amazing skill of the comrade that had saved their base.

On the ground they gathered together silently watching the emergency crews replenish their pods. No one spoke, the tragedy overpowering their minds.

The base commander approached, the huge fireball had been seen by all as well as being tracked by the sensors. "Report to command center," he said, seeing their shocked faces.

They followed him to base command and began to report the battle's difficult progress. "They far outnumber us but fortunately their pilots don't seem to be as well trained. We are barely holding our own. We must get back immediately." Logi reported and all the squadrons stood up to follow him to their pods, almost ready to fly out with renewed energy transmitters loaded in.

As he approached his pod, Vala came forward and walked beside him, her arm around his waist. She gave him a squeeze and a quick kiss as he climbed into the pod. "I put in an extra powerful receiver," she said, "It's one of the few we have left."

He nodded silently and began the preflight checks. The new receiver squawked and he started to say it didn't work when a faint voice that could barely be understood said. "Isn't anyone coming to get us?"

"Okhi!" he shouted, "Where are you?"

Shortly, rescue pods had brought back the wounded pilot and his gunner from the smashed pod that had catapulted off the doomed bomberpod. It had skated across the flat ice on the edge of the deep crevice that had trapped the bomber and fallen into a shallow crevice that had protected them from the explosion.

Despite Okhi's instance that he could fly again, he was taken to the base hospital to have his multiple injuries treated.

Chapter 28

The Aftermath

Lee sat on the chair beside Scott's sleeping figure and waved to Iluak sitting beside Akiak's bed. *Dear Gaia, thank you for saving him.*

Logi and Vala tiptoed in, "Will Scott be well by next week? It looks like all the fighting and cleanup will be over by then and we have the central park in Blue City reserved for our Bonding."

Scott opened his eyes and slid his encased left arm out, the fingers searching and enlacing with Lee's. "Of course, I'll be ready, I've waited too long already. Imagine Karlos' brother being your gunner! Where are they?"

Logi answered, "At the hospital with Okhi and then all our squadron's going to celebrate our victory. If the Silversuit squadron hadn't circled back and attacked the bombers from behind, we would have been overcome. Joana is arranging everything. We're going there after here. First Vala has something to tell you."

Vala brushed her hand over the blond hairs sprouting on her scalp, looked at Lee, and blushed. "There are more than 200 young people in Blue Ice City who have passed the minimum age for Bonding. Most of them are Silversons and daughters and we are sharing our Bonding ceremony with several of them. We get to be just behind you in the entrance march as we were the first couple to prove we were ready to Bond." She again looked at Lee. "There's something I need to show you but I don't know if you will like it."

Lee looked at her, "I can't imagine anything I won't like on this beautiful day. We've even been thinking of visiting the warm lands and seeing if the wild animals have come back. The bacteria didn't affect most of them. The podcasts show great forests covering many of the ancient's cities. Come on, show me something I won't like."

Vala stood up and slid her body suit down from her waist.

Lee and Scotty both drew in their breaths in surprise.

"You see, you are not happy because you are not the only ones with the silver tree that is on a Bonded Silverdaughter. That shows that Silversons and Daughters are also the heirs of the first Silversuiters and so are carrying the blood of the Saviour and the Mistress."

"Not happy?" L'ora exclaimed, "I'm delighted. I never wanted to be unique, I just want to live with Scotty and watch our children grow up without fear. Are you the only one?"

Vala smiled, "You don't know how relieved I am. I've been worried ever since Logi first saw it. All the Silverdaughters that Bonded with a Silverson have the Silver tree over their womb."

Lee laughed, "Then we should look for a beautiful deserted city and make our own Silver City. All of our children will be immune to the bacteria. Of course, not near the exile island where the remainder of the Teacher's army was sent. I wonder how they are doing being so out of shape. Their training must have been neglected for years. It was funny to see how fast most of them surrendered when they realized the size, conviction and training of the International Council's force with the Silversuiters supporting them."

Scotty squeezed Lee's hand. "First, after the Bonding, I want to take you away to some beautiful place for a few months, just you and me."

Lee smiled at him, "You and me and Cato, of course."

Logi broke in, "But first you have to visit all of the places in the world that sent warriors to the final battle. They all want to know you."

Scotty groaned, "There goes my dream."

Vala said, "Well, you'll be able to search for any of your family that the Consequentors might have rescued. With all the new people that have gathered here for the battle, I've found that the rescued ones have been hidden all over."

Attributions

Stairs In A Cave Stock Photo
By papaija2008, published on 15 November 2012
Stock Photo - image ID: 100113575
Link:http://www.freedigitalphotos.net/images/
Landscapes_g114-Stairs_In_A_Cave_p113575.html

About the Author

Beverley Blount lives in Mexico City and El Paso, Texas, where she has completed 30 years of training Montessori teachers in her schools. She is now consulting in schools in Mexico and the United States.

Under her pen name, B. Palma, she has written seven bilingual books for young adults, weaving her husband's tales of growing up on his family's haciendas with her own adventurous teens in the Mexican countryside.

Silversuit III is her first Science Fiction adventure book and Silversuit I and II will soon follow.

Blount had an eight page article published in the award winning centennial issue of the Montessori Life journal and two lead articles in The Kappan, the ADK International Teacher's Organization's biannual journal.

In 2008, the Mexican National Circle of Reporters awarded her their Golden Sun statuette for special educational merit.

In November 2013, her book *El Dorado* was awarded the "Worthy of Being Called "Excellent" Book Award 2013.

Her life's work THE BLOUNT GUIDE TO READING, SPELLING AND PRONOUNCING ENGLISH, 2ND EDITION, is being used in schools in Mexico City and the United States.